With a Rough Tongue

With a Rough Tongue

Femmes Write Porn

edited by Amber Dawn
and Trish Kelly

ARSENAL
PULP PRESS

VANCOUVER

WITH A ROUGH TONGUE
Copyright © 2005 by the authors

ARSENAL PULP PRESS
341 Water Street, Suite 200
Vancouver, BC
Canada V6B 1B8
arsenalpulp.com

The publisher gratefully acknowledges the support of the Canada Council for
the Arts and the British Columbia Arts Council for its publishing program, and
the Government of Canada through the Book Publishing Industry Development
Program for its publishing activities.

Cover design and illustration by Kim Kinakin, *www.kimkinakin.com*
Text design by Shyla Seller

Printed and bound in Canada

Library and Archives Canada Cataloguing in Publication

        With a rough tongue : femmes write porn / Amber Dawn, Trish Kelly
(eds.).

ISBN 1-55152-193-8

        1. Erotic stories, Canadian (English) 2. Short stories, Canadian (English)
3. Lesbianism — Fiction. 4. Canadian fiction (English) — Women authors.
5. Canadian fiction (English) — 21st century. I. Dawn, Amber II. Kelly, Trish

PS8323.L47W58 2005   C813'.0108353
C2005-904322-9

ISBN-13 978-1-55152-193-0

INTRODUCTION, PART ONE
There's No "I" in Pornography

Amber Dawn

Pornography made its debut in my life during the summer of 1982, when I was eight years old and I found a couple of crumpled magazines in a shoebox under the bed.

My story is not unique. Many people, irrespective of gender, have shared with me childhood memories of discovering the "secret stash" of magazines hidden in their parents' house; it seems the experience is as common as catching the chicken pox or being sent off to summer camp. Where my story often differs from others is the fact that my findings were not tucked away in a tool shed or locked in a desk drawer, but in my mother's bedroom. Nor was I sneaking a peek at images of softly-lit, open-legged, bare-breasted women; my mother's magazines were hard-core gay porn. At the time, I could not begin to appreciate the taboo-break-ing significance of a single, heterosexual, self-proclaimed feminist being a consumer of pornography and finding sexual pleasure in gay pornography withal. Instead, I remember feeling what may be shared by all young, ac-cidental porn-finders: simultaneous uneasiness and fascination.

Since then, I have maintained a close relationship with pornography. Some of my earliest sexual experiences coincided with awkward, yet thrill-ing "third base parties" or adolescent group screenings of adult films. I no longer remember a single image from those films I watched in my youth. I don't know if what I saw aroused me, but I know the experience of watch-ing them did.

In my early twenties, I held jobs in two opposing worlds: a non-profit feminist collective and the adult entertainment industry. When I use the word "opposing" I do not mean to say that feminism, nor collectives, are intrinsically in opposition to pornography; indeed, there are several feminist-porn collectives in existence today. However, at the time, many feminists responded to my participation in pornography with piteous looks and by giving me the standard speeches about the exploitation of women. Some of my feminist co-workers went as far as criticizing my long fingernails and the short skirts I wore to work, accusing me of dressing for the patriarchy; I don't believe any of the other collective members received criticisms of their personal appearance.

I did not get involved with porn to become exploited. My primary reason was the paycheque; I wanted a university education, an apartment in the city — things my class background hadn't given me access to. Adult entertainment was, and largely remains, the only industry where an uneducated young woman can make sizably more than her male counterparts. Besides the income, I found I was a good candidate for adult work; my emerging identity as a kinky femme lesbian granted me a kind of gusto for anything sexual and socially risqué, and in the 1990s I was not alone. I quickly located myself within a community of sex-radical, third-wave, queer feminists who passed no judgment on my occupation.

Given these circumstances, one would think my consumption of and participation in pornography would have been dilemma-free; the truth was, while I challenged the second-wave feminist attitude towards pornography, I didn't entirely disagree with it. I witnessed divisions of the adult entertainment industry that, I believe, did portray women in a commodified and even humiliating light. Gradually, I became discouraged by the frequent, mechanical lack of emotion in "girl-on-girl" porn, the underlying racism in interracial porn, and the subordination of youth in "barely legal" porn. And although working in adult entertainment was, at times, liberating and allowed me to be financially independent, I left the industry with a sour taste in my mouth.

Creating a dialogue about the grey area between the long-standing polarities of anti-porn feminism and anti-censorship sex-radicalism is a delicate matter. By the late nineties, being an *anti*-anti-porn feminist, while harbouring feelings of discontentment for much of the porn being produced, was exhausting me. On the one hand, I argued with my sex worker friends and colleagues about the types of roles we allowed for ourselves and encouraged boycotts of what I deemed "misogynist-themed porn." On the other hand, I continued to uphold pornography as a relevant, even crucial facet of life. Then one day, when I was beginning to think I no longer knew where exactly I stood on the issue, something happened that made my feelings a lot clearer: I discovered a picture of myself on the Internet. The shot was at least a year old, and featured me dressed in school girl-esque clothes, lying on my back with my legs in the air, without panties. I remembered the particularly easy photo shoot, the clean and comfortable studio near downtown where it was taken; there was nothing about the shoot or the photo itself that bothered me. But on this website a caption above my head read: "I'm a dumb slut. I want to be filled with your cum." It was like stumbling upon a *doppelgänger* or an evil twin. *This isn't me,* I thought. *This can't be me.*

This is the moment I realized the cause of all my uneasiness with the majority of pornography: it does not reflect who I am. I am drawn to porn because, like many others, I am aroused by sex and by watching sex, but most of it does not represent me as a feminist-minded, queer, kinky femme. I knew I had to stop impotently grumbling about the shortcomings of what we know to be pornography and join the trail-blazing efforts of the handful of queer women producing their own porn. Since then, I've done everything from organizing and performing in women and gender-queer sex cabarets to spending my phone-bill money on the latest issue of *On Our Backs* magazine in this pursuit.

Co-editing *With a Rough Tongue* has been a rewarding experience, one which has proven to me that our lives, our identities, and our sexuality can coexist with unabashed, hard-core pornography. How affirming it is to see unashamed, femme characters, like the flirty yet forward Chloe in Sara Graefe's "Butt Really" or Ducky DooLittle's aggressive femme protagonist who sexually overmasters a perverted, panty-stealing laundromat attendant in "Clean Panties."

Many stories in this anthology have much in common with pornography produced for a heterosexual male audience, such as desirable, feminine characters and quick and uninhibited sex, but at the same time they subvert these same porn traditions. For example, a hasty sexually liaison between a cab driver and a woman on her way home may sound like a familiar porn plot, but in Miss Cookie LaWhore's "A Free Ride," that woman is a punk-rock drag queen, who comes up against both gender and cultural taboos while pursuing her desires.

Additionally, a 200-pound butch dyke, like "Roy" in Diana Cage's highway masturbation story, "'73 Nova," is seldom seen in porn. A New York Stonewall anniversary riot as the backdrop to desperately passionate sex, as seen in "early '90s femme memory #1" by Leah Lakshmi Piepzna-Samarasinha, is equally uncommon. So while the stories provide "an easy thrill," they delve deeper into human diversity and express underrepresented queer desire and queer culture.

In the tender and exploratory fisting scene in "Fisherman," Nalo Hopkinson averts the fetishization of racialized bodies and race clichés so often assigned to people of colour in pornography. Alternatively, Hopkinson employs a truly human and intimate voice to narrate the action: "She two massive legs pinning my own big ones down, brown on brown. I see she cocoa pod pum-pum, spread open and glistening, going to brown at the edges. Lord, what a thing." Not only does Hopkinson write a respectful and arousing sex scene, she shows the authentic lives and hardships of her characters, and the personal and cultural barriers they must overcome to allow themselves to act on their desires.

This sentiment of authenticity and overcoming obstacles is echoed throughout the stories in this collection. When Trish and I undertook *With a Rough Tongue* we expected hot sex and we expected dignified sex. What was a surprise to us was the sense of personal triumph that these stories came to us with; the stories themselves, like the characters in them, have taken risks and succeeded at fulfilling their innermost desires. I am grateful to *Rough Tongue*'s contributors, all of whom have renewed my belief that as a queer femme I don't have to experience the disappointment that can come with porn — only the pleasure.

INTRODUCTION, PART TWO
How Riot Grrrl Made Me a Pornographer

Trish Kelly

In downtown Vancouver, Granville Street, once the main drag and enter-tainment district for the entire city, is now a place in transition. Ten years ago, the street was officially called Theatre Row for its many cinemas, but I suspect also for the cheap porn shops whose 25-cent peepshows still draw a steady audience. As Granville Street changes, awkward gela-terias and nightclubs bloom and fade in place of the theatres. In the last ten years, everything on this street has changed except the porn shops, which bear the same yellowed signs warning minors and those "offended by sexuality" to stay out.

Ten years ago, I was a third wave feminist: a Riot Grrrl. On my way to our weekly collective meetings, I walked past the porn shops on Granville and would fantasize about smashing my backpack through their windows. I felt antagonized by society's depiction of women in those porn shops and elsewhere, and I refused the objectified version of women's sexuality I saw offered to me.

During this same time, I travelled the Pacific Northwest performing spoken word at punk shows and running workshops on identity politics at Grrrl-run conventions. Remarkably, Riot Grrrl is probably the reason that I am now, ten years later, writing and reading queer porn.

It certainly wasn't an obvious path. Riot Grrrl was equal parts political movement and support group; but it wasn't a lesbian movement, nor was it consciously sexy. Primarily, Riot Grrrl was a movement for survivors. Nearly every girl I met through Riot Grrrl was an abuse survivor. Whether at the hands of a family member or boyfriend, we were all reliving or healing from some sort of assault on our autonomy, and we bonded on our common ground — our struggle to reclaim girlhood. With barrettes and knee highs, we demanded the right to be innocent and self-defining at the same time. In our zeal to reclaim our language and our bodies, we scrawled words like *Tattletale* and *Hussy* with permanent markers across our bellies. Many of us took to the stage or typewriters, documenting and providing testimony as we retooled the symbolism and language of girlness to suit our needs.

I don't know if Riot Grrrl was a revolution, but it was definitely a rebellion, a reclaiming of things that were being withheld from us by our abusers, or society at large. For some, the struggle was about "taking back the night"; for others, it meant picking up a skateboard or a microphone. For me, Riot Grrrl gave me permission to reclaim the femininity that I'd been taught was dangerous. It also gave me a social context and audience for the anger I felt about the passive, pretty creature that a girl was supposed to be.

I didn't see the connection between my femininity and desire until I grew out of Riot Grrrl and entered the queer community. As a Riot Grrrl, I had declared that my sexuality was not up for discussion. Any boy who involved himself with Riot Grrrls knew better than to comment on a Grrrl's body or outfit — because boys who did, became fodder for the next spoken word piece or song. But in the queer community, sexuality was a major defining point. I encountered butches and gender-variant people who paid attention to me because, even in a room full of women, I was considered girly. These people weren't shy about vocalizing their appreciation, and I found their frankness exciting. I discovered that, unlike the attention I had received from heterosexual men, this attention felt good, even arousing.

Compared to the confrontational tactics of Riot Grrrl, the femme identity was subtle, but it still served to challenge expectations of me as a woman. While the dresses and nail polish could be read as straight, or traditionally feminine, my assertiveness and potty mouth alerted even the most thick-headed straight man that something was different about this girl.

Language and "telling" continued to be important to me as a femme, and so I searched out queer literature that reflected the demanding, honest sexuality I felt entitled to. I found women's erotica collections. I'd had a peripheral understanding of the feminist and lesbian movements outside Riot Grrrl, but in these erotica collections, I found more resonance. Because of my experience with Riot Grrrl, I sensed that the writers and their intended audience were healing from many wounds, and I respected the articulate emotionality of those stories. But I didn't always find them hot. I sensed an underlying tone of apology, and a handling of material far more delicate than what my imagination craved.

I wanted to edit *With a Rough Tongue* because, like many of the girls I met through Riot Grrrl, I am a survivor, but I don't want to be treated like a widow at her husband's funeral. I want a passionate, graphic depiction of sex that doesn't ignore our struggle or turn my desire into a landscape metaphor. I wanted to see a collection of stories about sexy femmes whose sexuality is informed by their experience, who can want without apology.

I wanted a collection of smut for the girls who will tell you that the Granville Street porn shops are the cheapest places in town to buy Cuban-foot pantyhose, but not quality latex or harnesses. It's for readers who dream about the saucy lady with the fancy nylons and nasty mouth, and for femmes who read porn.

THROUGH WINTER SUN

Suki Lee

The snow spins away from the wheels of my car, and rises up in clouds of white dust; its presence is a spectre, mocking me. My throat catches, like it's a person I'm longing for. I miss the sensation of having its arms wrapped around me, being caught in its clutch; how it reached every part of me, slipping into every crevice until I surrendered to it absolutely. I miss that sweet oblivion.

But rather than dwell on the white powder's inviting call, I respond to my present situation, and separate my legs to allow the tongue that's between them more room to play. As I do, the tongue hungrily probes, flicking down the full length of my cunt, dwelling teasingly around my clit. My centre gathers, contracts, and pulls. I am hot. I am impatient. I could lose control of the car.

The vehicle careens down a hill. I grip the steering wheel. The tires pass roughly over gravel and snow, spinning over narrow patches of ice. My surroundings are as beautiful as the ecstasy between my legs. It's all thinly veiled by an unseen hazard, though the road is sheathed in the same icy snow as the trees.

Now the tongue laps harder. I sigh heavily, encouraging it, drawing it in. Hot air blasts from the vents. I struggle to keep my eyes on the road. My bare ass burns against the car's heated leather seat, wet with my cunt juice. I sit up to see past the snowflakes that rush and melt on the windshield. The woman whose head is between my legs, a stranger to me before this afternoon, adjusts to this awkward position. I gaze down at her momentarily. Her flicking pink tongue glistens with wetness. I watch the movement of her finely shaped jaw as she devours me. Her jaw line was among the qualities that initially attracted me to her.

While I continue to drive, her tongue continues to navigate me. I realize that she and I have yet to kiss. She went for my cunt immediately, pulling up my skirt, licking me. I take one hand off the steering wheel, reach down, and touch her face with my fingertips. I slip two fingers into her mouth. She alternates between lapping my clit and taking my fingers deep into her throat. The inside of her mouth is warm, soft, wet. Satisfied, I rest my hand on the steering wheel and lean back in my seat. There, now we've kissed, I think, even though it was only a kiss between my fingers and her mouth.

Just as I'm reaching the threshold before orgasm, an obstacle comes into view at top speed: a pickup truck jockeying for position on the narrow road we share. The oncoming vehicle forces me to move my knee from where it's cocked uncomfortably on the dash, which jostles her out of position. My body registers the shock of her withdrawal. I press my foot to the brake. The oncoming truck passes, making my car shake. I stop by the side of the road. I'm startled and then aroused as fingers pass between my inner thighs to touch the mouth of my cunt. In another moment, they push into me. Instinctively, my entire body rushes to meet them with a strong thrust, surrounding them. I start rocking in motion with her fingers. Now and again, I slide over the knuckles, taking them into me. In another moment, her hand will be inside me.

The car is filled with the rhythm of her breathing. I lean further back in the driver's seat and relax my body, opening myself. Snow unfurls on the windshield, and then is wiped away.

In another moment, I will come.

Seconds later, I hear Tess whining in the back seat. I'm startled by the sound. I'd completely forgotten that the dog was here. No doubt she's been observing this escapade unfold from the start.

We resume driving in silence. It's several more minutes before we reach our destination. When I get out of the car, the soreness between my legs tells me that I was just fucked, hard. It fills me with heat on this crisp winter day.

The wind rustles the few remaining leaves that still cling to a nearby tree. Ahead of us, my aunt's house is nestled into the base of a hill. A bird titters. Tess bounds towards me with childlike joviality. Her frame is so large and unwieldy that she looks as if she might knock me down. I stand my ground, feigning indifference, so Tess doesn't sense my uneasiness around her. She makes several running passes by me in a flurry of fur and snow. I understand that she's looking for some sort of acknowledgement. I give her a pat on the head.

Not far from Tess and me is Eve, the real estate agent I hired to sell my aunt's house. She looks different now that she's out of my car, out from between my legs. The rural setting suits her. She's dressed in snow boots, worn jeans, a down jacket, and a black toque.

I walk over to where she stands. When we were making arrangements over the phone, we agreed to go over the details of the house my aunt bequeathed to me. And now she's doing just that, pointing out the work that needs to be done on the century-old farmhouse: the veranda needs to be replaced, the roof apparently sprouts a lawn in summer, and the second storey's many windows draw in the cold during winter. Eve assures me that I shouldn't be worried about selling the house.

"Do I look worried?" I ask her.

"Actually, yes."

Although we've only known each other for a few short hours, she has perhaps gleaned something of me in that time. The worry that she sees is not about the sale of the house. It's rather my personal reason for being here, out of the city, to escape my one and only love: the tender white antidote that drives me wild: cocaine.

Being the executor of my aunt's will has coincided with my overriding desire to lead a clean life. Here, there is an evergreen forest. Its hue alters with every shifting shadow, somewhat like my mood. Here, I hope to find myself. If the drug comes after me — furious, malcontent, stomping its foot — it won't find me.

"Did you know your aunt well?" Eve's question breaks the silence between us as we walk into the house. The dog prompts her for a pat by pushing its nose into her hand.

"We were close, but it's actually been a few years since I saw her last," I reply, sidestepping the dog into the kitchen. I pick up the vague smell of cinnamon.

Being here reminds me of my aunt as she was, with her grey and white hair, and her familiar dress of blue verging on turquoise. There was a stutter in her step that made her right shoulder roll forward as she walked. The most distinctive feature about her was that she never went anywhere without her dog. Tess seemed more like an extension of her personality than her pet. I remember my aunt telling me that she found her love for lightning storms conflicting because they terrified Tess.

I look down at Tess now, sitting obediently, tipping her head back, and panting madly. The dog is lost without her master, and as improbable as it seems to me, I have inherited her.

Eve and I wander the main floor of the house. She is pointing out the old barn board covering the walls when I gasp at an image moving in a picture frame. A second later, I realize that it's my reflection in a mirror. I'm seeing myself with clarity for the first time in a while: brown eyes, dark and deeply shadowed; an oval-shaped face, now rather thin; a red lipstick-smudged mouth, the result of biting my lip in the car. I'm drawn in by this sober look at myself.

"Beautiful," Eve whispers in my ear.

I flush at being caught in this seemingly narcissistic moment.

"Are you always so charming?" I ask her reflection.

"No, if you want to know the truth."

I shoot her a sideways glance. Eve's already close enough to kiss me. And then she does, pushing her tongue into my mouth. Mine slides over hers and I taste my cunt, still fresh in her mouth from our tryst in the car. I take her jacket off and run my hands up her bare arms. I undo the top button of her pants, then slip my hand into her wet pussy. She does the same to me. We finger each other's clits, holding the other captive, moving our fingers. Face to face, we pass through stages of arousal: "I want your cunt juice on my tits."

"I want you to slip your tongue into me."

"I want to fuck you with my cock."

With this last statement, she throws her head back. I find her so beautiful: hay-coloured hair shaved close, green eyes, black eyelashes, and a full, voluptuous mouth. Riding her cunt with my finger, I work her faster and harder, kneading her cunt viciously. She quickly becomes liquid against my touch and collapses against my arm. Her knees buckle to the floor. With a pained expression, she comes to me, her sounds of pleasure filling the house.

Afterwards, we lean shoulder to shoulder against the wall. I turn and find her staring at me.

"Do I look like your girlfriend?" I ask.

"I don't have one."

"You're attracted to me," I say.

"Yes, but that's not it either."

"You're avoiding other work you have to do."

"Yes, but that's not it."

I lift my hands. "Help me then."

"It's just you," she says.

"What?" I ask, folding my hands against themselves and slipping them between her legs.

"It's just you."

She touches my lips.

"Well," I murmur, holding onto the words, not knowing what else to say. "Well, that's something."

I take some time to inspect the small house on my own. Its walls are crooked and layered with years of paint and wallpaper. The rooms are small. It has a cottage-like feeling. I walk up the creaky wooden stairs to the second floor. Bright light shimmers through the window ahead of me, illuminating the space in narrow shafts. Looking out, I see a large hill that leads away from the house and gradually ascends to a tree-covered mountain. It is beautiful here, and I have a perfect view of Eve below.

She's speaking to Tess, who sits obediently in the snow, awaiting a command. Suddenly, the dog walks in a circle and then crouches and barks, as if they've done this before. The two lunge, intertwine, and grapple to the snowy ground.

A sensation of arousal in me intervenes, as Eve rises from the wrestle, full of vigour. She looks up and sees me watching her. Something flashes in her eyes. I interpret it as permission.

I call Tess into the house. She rushes in and sits at my feet, poised, staring unflinchingly at me. I ruffle her ears before going out to Eve.

Eve and I are still very much strangers. Despite that, I uncross her arms and lead her by the shoulders and towards the car. I look into her eyes.

"Are you scared?" I ask.

"No," she answers reflexively.

She runs her hands beneath my sweater, down the curve of my abdomen. I slowly undo the zipper of her jeans. Eve shivers. She's wearing men's underwear. It's snowing lightly. Snowflakes land on her belly and melt. Slowly, very slowly, I pull down her underwear. She's entirely shaven. With two fingers, she spreads herself for me.

"Come closer," she says.

I kneel in the snow.

At the very crux of her is the glistening moon of a clitoris.

I bring my tongue over Eve's bald pussy, licking the warmth of her. Eve responds by thrusting against me. I take this as her command. While continuing to lick her clit, I separate her lips and push my fingers into her wet warmth, thrusting them upwards. The cold numbs my knees. Eve spreads her legs. She stretches her arms out to brace herself against the car. I look up and see that she's shuddering from the cold. I brush my hand across her nipples; they are hard and stiff. I squeeze one of them. Eve gasps. I release her and move my hand across her body and behind her. Her ass is cold from the winter air. And because of the cold and because I'm fucking her and licking her clit and she's so open to me, her body gives me permission: I probe a finger up her ass. She takes everything in, and leans her head back against my car. I fuck her pussy until she comes to me and her calls echo into the forest.

It only seems odd that Eve is going to leave on horseback when I'm standing there with the dog, wishing her goodbye. The moment is too strange to be awkward. Our kiss is rough.

We had agreed that she could have the horse in place of commission for selling my aunt's house. I thought this appropriate since she had an existing relationship with it. Eve had been exercising the animal when my aunt's arthritis made it too difficult for her to ride. She'd continued doing so after my aunt passed away. Now, with both our signatures on the legal agreement, she's taking the animal with her to its new home, which is apparently only a five-minute car ride away.

Eve mounts the horse. I look at the stirrup, wishing that I could mount too. I'd fuck her from behind, reaching down between her legs as the horse carried us through the woods.

But now, the beast stomps impatiently in the snow. Eve says goodbye back to me and falls into the horse's rhythm naturally, riding Western-style with one hand relaxed loosely on her jeans and the reins gathered up in the other. The horse transitions smoothly from a walk to a canter and soon both horse and rider disappear, and I am alone.

It becomes dark quickly. The wind pushes against the house. I spend the rest of the evening at the wood stove burning two decades of utility bills that my aunt had filed in banker's boxes. Stacks of *National Geographic* magazines likewise meet a similar fate, as do three-foot-high piles of newspapers I find in the basement. The flame is so hot that I'm able to warm soup on it. I eat directly from the pot, watching the flames flick from the stove. I find the moment quietly symbolic, and take it to represent the end of my self-medicating drug use.

I'm mesmerized by the flame that burns in yellows and browns and blues. I have a strong craving. To crave is familiar, but instead of cocaine, I'm now consumed by the pressing need to push my fingers into wetness. I repeatedly imagine Eve on her back, and me thrusting into her. I can think of nothing else. As an antidote to this fantasy, I go to the couch, lie on my stomach, finger my clit, and ride it as if I'm between Eve's legs. And although I'm touching myself, I feel fully and bodily on her. I swear as I come.

The evening continues to pass as I pack books and clothing. I drink a lot of coffee and savour how it elevates me to a high and then how it makes me plummet. Now and again, I ask Tess whether I should retain certain objects for posterity, World War II ration cards and my aunt and uncle's marriage certificate among them. Although the dog shows no interest, I decide to save them from the fire.

It is strange to be newly clean. It is divine in a way. Now and again, I walk outside onto the porch wearing only slippers and a sweater. The cold rushes against my skin, shocking my body. Snow whirls at my feet. I couldn't possibly hear if someone were approaching me through the howls and whistles. Although I'm not usually fearful, I bring the portable phone as a precaution. I realize the absurdity of it, but I'm unaccustomed to being on my own, and even less so to being in the country.

On my last walk outside before going to bed, the phone rings in my hand.

"It's me," the voice says on the end of the receiver. "Are you finding the house cold?"

"Not at all. It's sweltering, actually."

"I'm sure."

Rather than spend more time in discussion, I extend an invitation for Eve to stay the night. I try not to think of it as a date, although this is somewhat difficult when she arrives on horseback. My gallant cowboy appears in the shadows outside the living room window.

She lets herself into the house, stomping the snow off her boots. I listen to her footsteps along the creaky floor as I wait for her, naked, laid out on blankets over the rug. My legs are spread wide. My hands open my cunt to her. The sound of the roaring fire fills the room.

Eve kneels. Her skin is cold, and exudes the strong smell of horse. She's wearing a different shirt from earlier today — this one is torn at the shoulder. Her arms are muscular and strong. I study them, and choose the place where I will bite down on her later.

"Fuck me." I lean towards her. My stomach quivers.

"I want your tits first."

Eve leans down and puts her mouth on my nipples, which harden quickly. She slides her cold fingers inside me, reaching deeply. The sensation sends off a mixture of sensations at once shocking and satisfying. A huge yellow flame climbs out of the wood stove. Eve's tongue laps at the medallions of my nipples.

"Are you always attracted to strangers?" I question, whispering in her ear.

Eve glances up while continuing to fuck me. "My instinct tells me what to like."

"What else do you like?"

"Shiny objects."

"Like coins?" I suggest.

"Like your necklace."

Eve takes it into her mouth and bites my neck. At the same time, she withdraws her hand slowly from between my legs. My cunt relinquishes her unwillingly.

"Please," I plead. I'm impatient and want her in me. She sits back calmly and undoes her zipper. I lean forward, pull up her shirt, and feed on her nipples. They wake to my tongue. Eve sighs deeply. I'm on the edge, and this brings me closer. My eyes closed, I feel Eve's hand on the back of my head, then I'm suddenly being pushed down. A long erect shaft brushes against my lips, and I'm pushed down again. I open my mouth and the cock thrusts in. It withdraws slowly. I open my eyes and see the transparent tip of a condom over the dildo's head. I grip the dildo and take it in again. This time I control its journey, pulling it in and pushing it out of my mouth while looking up at her.

Eve gradually draws her dick from my mouth. I lie back and watch as she slowly spreads lube over the length of the dildo. She squeezes some onto her hands and slips them inside me. We both know that I'm ready to take her. Eve pulls out her hands, places the head of her cock at the mouth of my cunt, and slowly slides it in. I'm so open that my body accepts the full length of her shaft, which she pushes into me until her body's flush with mine. The cock fills me. I drive my cunt up against her, plunging her deep into me, bucking her, forcing her to follow my rhythm. She does, leaning into me, thrusting quickly, riding me the way I want her to. While she's fucking me, I watch her pupils grow wide as she takes in my open-mouthed pleasure. Seconds later, I go off, coming from my very depths. Eve continues thrusting into me rapidly. My orgasm climbs to a scream.

Afterwards, she lies on top of me, and licks the sweat from my neck. We devour each other with deep kisses. The air is cold when we finally rise and find our way upstairs to bed, where we collapse, fully sated. Eve feeds briefly on my nipples, but soon falls asleep. Her breath is hot against my neck.

Late into the night, I lie on my back watching the ceiling. I am awake and frustrated that sleep isn't coming. My heart pumps. My senses are more alert than usual. The house sighs occasionally from the winter wind. The floors creak of their own accord. I listen to Eve's breath.

When sleep finally comes, my mind contemplates what it would be like to be a man — or rather, what it would be like to have a cock. In the dream, I see Eve and I push myself into her mouth, then I turn her onto all fours, shove my cock into her wet hole, and fuck her hard from behind.

The next morning, I wake to the strong winter wind. A vague feeling from the previous night comes to me. My body is delightfully slick. I look down at my nipples. They've hardened in the cool morning air. I look farther down between my legs. I remember my dream. I stretch my arm across the sheets and touch Eve.

She's still sleeping, and so it's easy for me to reach over to her side of the bed and take the dildo that lies there. I roll her onto her back and slip it inside her. She wakes, then takes me in as if that's what she's been waiting for all night. We fuck to the point of exhaustion, then collapse onto the mattress. My hand touches the sweat on her back. We kiss until our lips are raw then fall asleep again.

When I wake, it's with a start. I'm in bed alone. I put on some pyjamas and rush downstairs. My voice echoes in the house as I call the dog's name, but I don't hear her padding canine feet. I throw on a coat, shove my feet into boots, and rush out the door.

I spy the dog in the distance, running across the field. She bounds, kicking snow up behind her. "Tess!" I call after her. But then suddenly I'm grabbed from behind and taken to the ground. My pyjamas are pulled down. The snow shocks my skin. I scream. I strain to look up through the bare branches of trees at the winter sun. I am out of my element, unable to get off the ground. I brace myself.

In this moment, the thought occurs to me that I will stay here for a while. It's so real and true that I know I will do it. It warms my skin as much as the hot, wet tongue that's working its way furiously all over my cunt.

BUTT REALLY

Sara Graefe

Girls often mistook Chloe for the shy, quiet type. She was soft-spoken by nature, and had a tell-tale pink flush that would rise to her cheeks whenever anyone flirted with her.

But as Billy was beginning to discover, Chloe was the kind of femme who knew what she wanted and how to get it. It was one of the things that made Billy mad about her, and Chloe knew it.

"Nice ass," Billy said appreciatively, patting Chloe's butt as she sashayed oh-so-innocently in front of her on the sidewalk in her tight little skirt. "Nice ass," she said again later in bed, as Chloe lounged next to her on her stomach, oh-so-casually displaying her nicely toned derrière. Billy caressed it gently with her hand, sending tingles through Chloe's buttcheeks.

"Mmmm," Chloe murmured, drinking it in, her ass melting like butter under Billy's fingers.

They'd been seeing each other for a couple of weeks. They'd fucked a number of times, always at Billy's place because Billy liked to run the show. She wasn't a stone butch by any stretch of the imagination; she was sweet, soft, and gentlemanly, but nonetheless a butch who got wet from giving a woman pleasure — if not wetter than receiving it herself. Chloe clued into this pretty quick, because Billy would come spontaneously whenever Chloe reached orgasm. And Chloe would lie back on the bed, spread her legs, and let Billy have her way with her.

What Billy didn't realize was that Chloe was biding her time, testing her. *Can she top me enough?* Billy, meanwhile — forever the gentleman — was taking things slow with her new girl. It had been a few dates and Chloe hadn't even seen Billy's dick yet. *Maybe she isn't into accessories?* Chloe wondered. But Billy didn't want to blow her wad all at once, and Chloe was content to wait. Billy's hand had a way of slipping into her cunt so sweetly, and she'd make Chloe dance for hours on the tip of her tongue. Dick or no dick, Billy kept passing test after test with flying colours, and Chloe decided it was time to crank the volume up a notch.

"Why don't you come over to my place tonight?" Chloe breathed into Billy's ear that Friday, over the phone. "I'll make you dinner."

Billy was surprised by her offer. To date, she'd never set foot in Chloe's apartment, an artsy live-work loft on the east side of town. Usually she'd simply swing by in her Jeep to pick Chloe up, ringing the buzzer outside the building. Chloe always liked to keep her waiting, just for a few minutes, before flouncing out in a pretty outfit. Billy was more than a little intrigued by the proposition of dinner — and even though she wasn't an old-school butch, she relished the idea of her femme cooking specially for her. "Sure," she said. "Sounds good."

"Great. I'll see you at seven."

Chloe hurried home from work that afternoon. She plumped the cushions on the couch, dimmed the lights, and put on a sultry jazz CD. She jumped into the shower, humming to herself as the warm spray cascaded over her naked body. She closed her eyes as she soaped her breasts and her backside. She grew wet with anticipation as she imagined Billy's hands resting there, later, caressing her behind. She lingered over the open lingerie drawer, carefully picking through satin and lace, garter belts and g-strings, agonizing over what to wear. *Everything has to be just right....*

By the time Billy buzzed downstairs, Chloe had transformed herself. She'd carefully laced herself into a cream boned corset over a short, brown leather skirt that hugged her ass. Her long, honeyed hair softly framed her face, the wavy tips caressing her bare shoulders. She *tick-tick-ticked* over the hardwood to the intercom in her high heels, the seams on her stockings running up her deliciously long legs.

"Hi, gorgeous girl," she sang playfully into the handset. "Come on in."

Billy stepped into the elevator holding a bouquet of long-stemmed red roses, taking a deep breath before she pressed the button for the third floor. It was her first time on Chloe's turf and, though she hated to admit it, she was actually feeling a little nervous. She caught her reflection in the elevator wall as she rode up. She ran her fingers through her blonde, boyish hair, and checked herself out. She was sporting a sleek black shirt with a zip-down collar that she'd bought specially for the occasion, freshly pressed chinos, and her favourite pair of boots, black Blundstones polished till they gleamed. She hoped she looked good without looking like she'd made an *effort* to look so good — which, of course, she had.

Standing outside Chloe's door, Billy raised her hand to knock, but suddenly the door whipped open and Chloe pulled her inside. Billy took in Chloe's new look and inhaled sharply, but before either of them could utter a word, Chloe pinned Billy against the wall of the vestibule with a deep, long kiss. Billy could barely process what was happening. She felt her body giving over, her tongue meeting Chloe's as it hungrily probed her mouth, her clit snapping to attention below as Chloe pressed up against her pubic bone.

Chloe came up for air, leaving Billy breathless and at a loss for words. "Wow," Billy finally managed. "Good to see you, too."

"Just a little taste to whet your palate," Chloe teased, eyes sparkling. She ran a finger suggestively down Billy's chest. "You hungry?"

Billy grinned. "Ravenous," she replied, playing along. "I've hardly eaten all day."

"Good."

Billy was still holding the flowers, now a bit squished after their initial encounter. "These are for you," she said, handing them over as she tried to fight the blush that was rising in her cheeks. What was going on? Usually she wasn't so damn flustered.

Chloe picked up on this and smiled to herself. *So far, so good.* "Thank you," she said, accepting the bouquet. "They're beautiful." She leaned over and gave Billy another lingering kiss. "I'd better put these in water," she announced, and sashayed down the hall towards the kitchen, her ass swaying gently under the sleek brown leather. "Come on in and make yourself comfortable," she called back over her shoulder.

Billy didn't need an invitation. She followed Chloe down the hall, not sure if she was able to wait till after dinner to rip that little skirt off

Chloe's hips. But it was her first time at Chloe's, and Billy decided to mind her manners.

"Nice place," she said, admiring the high ceilings and large windows that looked out over the street. The whole space was aglow in soft candlelight.

"Thanks," Chloe called from the kitchen area, arranging the roses in a crystal vase. "I just love it here."

Billy noted a spiral staircase leading to a small loft area upstairs, which she assumed was Chloe's bedroom. She craned her neck for a better look just as Chloe reappeared with a glass of red wine.

"Dinner will be ready in a sec," Chloe told her, handing her the glass. She sauntered back to the kitchen, aware of Billy's eyes on her as she bent over the stove to stir the sauce, her ass tilted invitingly in Billy's direction.

Billy shook her head and grinned. *There she goes again.* "That looks delicious," Billy said, coming up behind Chloe and wrapping her arms around her waist, pulling her in so that Billy's cunt rubbed up against Chloe's crack.

"Mmmm," Chloe murmured, her ass contracting with pleasure against Billy's hard clit. "You want a taste?"

She reached over the counter towards a set of expensive cooking implements which dangled on hooks from a large stainless steel rack. There was a whole assortment of ladles, spoons, spatulas, and devices that Billy had never seen before.

"You certainly have all the tools of the trade," Billy said.

"I don't mess around," Chloe assured her, selecting a large serving spoon. "In fact," she added, "I have a bit of a fetish. Always have to have the latest toy." She dipped the spoon into the pasta sauce, a tomato pesto with Portobello mushrooms. "Are you into toys, Billy?" She turned around to face her, holding the spoon full of sauce enticingly in front of Billy's lips. The aroma of basil and rosemary wafted up, teasing Billy further.

"Toys?" Billy felt herself blushing again. *What is wrong with me?* she thought. Of course, Billy liked toys. She'd have strapped her dick on tonight if she'd known Chloe was going to be so forward. "Well," Billy started to stammer, but before she could get the words out, Chloe gently slid the spoon into her mouth.

The sauce spread over her tongue like warm, liquid velvet, the rich flavours exploding on her tastebuds. "Mmmm...." She closed her eyes and positively swooned.

"Glad you like it," Chloe whispered into her ear, brushing past her to the cupboards. She bent over, cocking her butt coyly in the air as she reached for a serving dish from one of the lower shelves. The corset slid up, exposing the small of Chloe's back and a hint of her underwear — cream lace, to match the corset.

Billy gasped. Chloe looked up at her and smiled. "What?" she asked innocently, but now she was blushing like mad too. She knew damn well she was driving Billy crazy, and was enjoying every last second of it.

"You know what."

"I don't have a clue what you're talking about." Chloe walked by and bent over again, this time right in front of Billy, opening the drawer under the stove. Billy looked down and could see that Chloe was in fact wearing a little lace thong that rode up her crease as she leaned over. Billy swallowed hard, fighting the sudden urge to grab the spatula from the rack and spank Chloe's flirty little ass.

"Excuse me," Chloe sang, tray in hand, brushing past Billy again. But Billy couldn't take it anymore. She grabbed Chloe, whirled her around, and pinned her up against the fridge.

"You little minx," Billy breathed into Chloe's ear, cupping her left breast and squeezing it hard. "You're asking for it."

Chloe's heart started to pound, and she tingled all the way down to her clit. But she played it cool as she casually removed Billy's hand: "Not so fast. You'll spoil your dinner." She reached for Billy's crotch, and began to stroke her there gently, back and forth. She could feel Billy clenching through her khakis. "Unless you'd like to start with dessert."

Billy let out a low moan, giving over to Chloe's touch.

Chloe continued to tease her cunt. "Is that a yes?"

"Yes."

"Are you going to ask me nicely?"

The hairs on the back of Billy's neck bristled. "Please."

"Please, what?" Chloe was enjoying this. It was as though they'd totally flipped roles.

"Please, Chloe, let's start with dessert." A pool was forming in Billy's pants. This little game of switcheroo was turning her on, too.

"Come on then," Chloe whispered, taking Billy by the hand and leading her up the spiral staircase to the loft. She sat Billy down on the lush purple duvet that covered the double bed. Without a word, she slowly unzipped Billy's shirt. She reached in and found Billy's breasts, fondling each one in turn, teasing the nipples until they sprang erect between her thumb and forefinger. Chloe felt her own butt cheeks tighten, her cunt moisten with anticipation. "Take your shirt off," she said.

Billy complied, lifting the black garment over her head, exposing her voluptuous upper body.

"Good girl," Chloe said. She got to her feet and began to strip for Billy, slowly and methodically unlacing the corset, exposing her perky little breasts. She slid off her skirt, revealing a lacy, cream garter belt, and of course, the thong riding up her tight little butt. She deliberately lingered over her garter belt, taking her sweet time to unhook each stocking and slide it down her legs, just to prolong Billy's agony.

"You like that?" Chloe asked, knowing full well that Billy did.

"Yes." Billy reached for her hungrily, but Chloe backed away.

"Not so fast." She took out some matches and lit some candles on the dresser. "You never answered my earlier question."

Billy was thrown. "What question?"

Chloe flashed a knowing little smile then reached under the bed and pulled out a shiny pink toolbox. "Are you into toys, Billy?" she repeated, plunking the box down right between Billy's legs. Chloe leaned over and grabbed Billy's crotch, groping about with her fingers. "Do you have a big dick somewhere that you haven't told me about?"

Billy gasped. "Yes."

"Where is it?" Chloe demanded, rubbing hard and fast now against Billy's clit.

"At home," she stammered. "I didn't think you were ready."

"I've always been ready," Chloe assured her. "If you're a good girl, maybe I'll let you borrow one of mine."

She released Billy's clit, leaving it aching for more as she popped open the toolbox. But of course, this was no ordinary toolbox; it was filled with silicone dills, vibes, double dongs, you name it, all different shapes, sizes, and colours, and about five different kinds of lube. In the little containers meant for nails and screws, she'd tucked latex gloves and dental dams. Billy sucked in her breath. She couldn't believe her eyes.

"Like I said, I have a bit of a fetish for tools," Chloe said. "I have a growing collection."

"I can see that," Billy replied. At the rate Chloe was going, she could open her own sex shop; and to think Billy had been giving Chloe time before introducing her dick into the relationship.

Chloe lifted the top tray of the toolbox and pulled out a delicate little g-string triangle harness of purple leather with black feathers. "This little number is mine," she announced, laying it on the bed. Indeed, it was the perfect harness for a femme. Billy couldn't wait to see it on her. But show and tell wasn't over just yet; Chloe was busy retrieving another harness from the toolbox, a sturdier model with thicker, black leather straps. "And I reserve this one for my favourite butches." She threw it at Billy. "Put it on."

Chloe didn't need to ask twice. Billy grinned crookedly as she slid off her chinos and boy briefs, stepped into the harness, and tightened the straps.

"Now I'd like you to pick your dick," Chloe instructed.

Billy was blushing again; she couldn't help it. She'd never known a femme with a dick, let alone an entire collection, and she'd most certainly never strapped on any other than her own.

"Go on," Chloe urged her, enjoying this. "Don't be shy." Billy glanced through the toolbox, weighing her options. "You can touch them if you want," Chloe offered.

Billy picked up a thick blue dick with a textured surface. It flopped in her hand as she handled it — *nah, too soft.* She liked her dick to be good and hard. She reached back into the box and — surprise — pulled out a curvaceous, purple Venus figurine. *Nah, too femmy, too PC, or both.* She finally settled on a long, black, semi-realistic model that thickened towards the base — *just right.* All this time, Billy was aware of Chloe's eyes on her, intently watching her every move. Billy looked up and gave her a wry smile. "This one's kinda like mine," she explained, slipping it through the opening in the harness.

"Nice," Chloe said, assessing her. She wrapped her hand around Billy's big dick, squeezing it up and down the shaft. Billy sighed with pleasure as the base ground into her clit. "You going to fuck me nicely?"

"Yes," Billy promised. She thrust her hips forward, sliding her dick between Chloe's legs, brushing against her lips. "I want you to get on the bed and spread your legs for me."

"I know you do, baby, but really...." Chloe admonished, playing with her.

"What?" Billy was confused.

"There's one more thing." Chloe reached back into the bottom of the toolbox and pulled out what looked like a small, slender silicone dill with a rounded tip. She waved it in the air with a flourish. "The *pièce de résistance*."

"What is it?" Billy wanted to know.

"What do you think it is?" Chloe threw back at her playfully, inserting a mini-vibrator into the base of the toy. "Come on, I'll show you."

Chloe climbed onto the bed. This was the moment she'd been waiting for. Billy expected her to lie on her back and spread her legs, but instead she carefully got onto her hands and knees, tilting her ass in the air — an offering. She looked over her shoulder at Billy, and their eyes locked. Billy nodded — she'd figured as much. Chloe smiled and silently handed over the toy.

Billy sank down next to Chloe and began stroking her rear, kissing it. Chloe's butt muscles started to clench and unclench with pleasure.

"Nice ass," Billy said, as always.

"Mmmm," Chloe murmured. As Billy kept kneading her bum, waves of warmth spread over her entire posterior. Her cheeks rose hungrily to meet Billy's touch, greedy for more.

"Such a naughty little ass," Billy observed, slapping it. Chloe giggled, feeling the reverberations all the way to her clit. Then she felt Billy's finger, slowly tracing circles around her anus. Chloe inhaled sharply with anticipation. "It's so naughty I think I should fuck it."

"Yes," Chloe breathed, her voice now a whisper. "Please."

Billy was making circles with the butt dill now. Chloe could feel the smooth, lubed tip caressing her hole. She sighed with pleasure. Billy started probing gently with the dill, pressing in and out of Chloe's tight little opening, marvelling at the strength of Chloe's muscles guarding that most vulnerable orifice. Billy's crotch started to pound under her harness. She was pleasantly surprised by just how much she was getting off on this.

"I've never actually fucked a woman up the ass before," Billy confided. "I've never been with a woman who could take it."

"I can take anything from you," Chloe pleaded. She was so hungry for it, which made Billy all the more wet. Billy then took a breath and pushed the dill through the invisible barrier — it was as though Chloe had suddenly opened up and let her in. Chloe moaned as Billy penetrated her; a deep, intense moan, the likes of which Billy had never heard before, from the core of Chloe's being, as though Chloe were letting Billy into some secret, hidden part of her self.

"You like that?" Billy asked, slowly, rhythmically, fucking her ass, back and forth, back and forth.

"Yes," Chloe managed, as the dill pounded into her rectum, sending waves of intense pleasure throughout her body. Billy turned on the vibe, and Chloe was nearly beside herself as the tingling intensified, running through each nerve ending of her ass, right into her clit, as though they were hardwired together. With each thrust, Chloe was being transported to another zone, a whole other plane of existence, and she was taking Billy there with her, Billy could feel it. It was the hottest thing, and Billy was honoured to be along for the ride. There was something so raw about it — this unbridled passion emanating from Chloe's being. Chloe was giving off heat; Billy could practically see it rising off her body.

Then without warning, Chloe leaned back and straddled Billy's dick with her cunt. Billy gasped as Chloe's weight bore down on her clit through the harness. Chloe rode Billy's dick with her back arched, and her long, wild mane waving madly behind her, as Billy continued to fuck her ass. Billy held tight to the butt dill and moaned as the base of the dick slammed into her labia, making her wetter by the second. The reverberations from the butt toy travelled through Chloe's cunt, all the way down Billy's shaft to her clit, sending Billy to new heights of her own. Chloe rode and rode Billy like that, as Billy rammed sweetly into her cunt, and plunged deep up her ass.

"Are you going to come with me?" Billy grunted, not able to hang on much longer.

"Yes," Chloe managed, "yes...."

Chloe's whole body tensed, and then released. Suddenly she was spraying everywhere, all over Billy's hand and big dick. Billy came too, gushing under her harness. Chloe was practically sobbing, her body rocking with the most intense orgasm Billy had ever witnessed. Billy removed the plug, turned off the vibe, and took Chloe in her arms.

"You delicious fuck," she said, holding Chloe tight as she shuddered with the aftershocks.

"Thank you," Chloe murmured, eyes half-closed. "That was exactly what I needed."

Yup, Billy thought. *She's definitely a femme who knows what she wants.*

They lay like that together for awhile in each other's arms, enjoying the afterglow. The smell of long-forgotten pasta sauce wafted up the stairs, and Billy's stomach growled.

"Oh my God," Chloe exclaimed, suddenly remembering. "Dinner. You must be starving."

She was about to leap out of bed, but Billy stopped her.

"Dinner can wait," Billy insisted. She grinned mischievously, and reached for the butt dill. "I'd like some more dessert, please."

early '90s New York femme memory #1
Leah Lakshmi Piepzna-Samarasinha

In the abandoned warehouse of my imagination, you press your thigh hard
between mine. As I suck my breath in deep, I can smell rotting drywall and
the pit toilet dug in back on the first floor, a million beer cans and piss
buckets. Your hands on my bare thighs push my short skirt up and I arch
my back so my neck is in just the right place for your teeth.

In this memory we're still twenty-one, you didn't die, this neighbourhood hasn't been gentrified yet. There is no hipster mall or locks for the
bathroom doors, just the sound of the BQE rushing past my left ear and
nobody on the Mad Max streets for days. Just millions of empty roofs
to fuck on, fall asleep on, huddled under army blankets preparing for
revolution, coming to as the sun sears its way up at five in the morning,
or rain coming down like pebbles in the face as you're curled up in your
animal tangle under the blankets. Cool but swearing and stumbling your
way down the steps to the hot-as-fuck third floor. New York still smells
like old piss everywhere. Outside the room I hold on to at 2nd and B, guys
are still lined up every few feet with their hands out, muttering *poison,
poison*, letting all the regulars pass by. The angel of death is tagged above
the doorway of the methadone clinic.

I want to go back there, to that time before condos and sushi restaurants, people selling green velvet armchairs and postcards for twenty cents
on the street, two-dollar breakfast specials, walking back from Clit Club
at three in the morning, crossing the city from the Meatpacking District to
the Lower East Side, freezing winters in a garter belt and fishnets, boiling
hot summers in a bra and bomber jacket, hanging out on the stoop. You
and me and tomorrow's revolution: girls squatting in the apartment run-

ning a third-world women's magazine in 1995, a riot without a permit. Us brown glinting girls in our overalls and silver pendants between the tits, your thick braids corn-rowed down, red doo rag. "Boy" wasn't in the vocabulary yet, but you were boy enough to the fellas down the block catcalling you or slapping hands. You were boy and girl enuf to me.

Baby, you hiss, still talking smooth, your hand on my hips making them melt to burnt brown sugar. It's the night of Stonewall twenty-five and we're running up the alleys, from the drag march by Tompkins to the ragged anarchist march by the West Side Highway. *Stonewall was a riot, not a fucking brand name.* Throwing rocks and screaming, and running from the cops who swell from nowhere. The fucking International Socialists grab the megaphone trying to "direct" us, but separating us in fifteen different ways. You shimmy up a streetlight to look above the crowd and don't see that girl you fucked once in a while, what was her name, that skinny blonde bitch with the huge tit rings. We're nonmonogamous sex radicals, but I still hate her. My hips are too sore to follow, so I stand there in my slip and combat boots with a twenty of Pete's in a brown paper bag (or maybe this is the year that Colt 45 sells for ninety-nine cents a bottle). Dusky sunset skin, throwing back bottles and tear gas canisters. Split up, split up. But after the protest had been dispersed, we still make it back in front of the Stonewall, cobblestones that had been soaked in the blood of Puerto Rican and Black transwomen, femmes, and butches like us. We start dancing, taking off our shirts, naked in our boots and fishnets, shaved heads, your soft braids, my long curls and tits. Not even the Jersey frat boys, their jaws dropped, staring at titties could ruin this night.

Walking home past 13th Street's squat row, down B to Houston to Canal to the Williamsburg Bridge. That little hut halfway up the wide wooden promenade of the pedestrian walkways, all boarded up and covered with graffiti. The old works in a pile and the smell of burnt toast from the Dominos' sugar factory across the river. Hot night, our shirts only just back on. You pull me behind the wall, we push and shove each other around a bit, the wind whips by and there's a three-hundred-foot drop over the edge. We wrestle; you try to pin me but I'm slippery and wiry for my skinny. I squirm out from under you, flip over, and pin you down with my big, strong thighs. *Don't be bitchy*, I murmur. I sit up straight and pin my hair and grind my cunt through my slip down on you. You moan and curse, *I'm not gonna let you in, not this time.* I slide around, as smooth as you, and push you back.

I don't say I know you'll let me fuck you. There's always that moment when electricity hovers, threatening to strike, but I always find the pathway through that smoggy tunnel full of stars. You tense for a second until I roll you on your side, ass up, boy shorts caught around your knees, and I move like there's no reason why you would say no. Your jaw clenches, unclenches, I snap a finger against your clit, once, twice, three times. Tap your ass, flick against your asshole. You moan into concrete. *Yeah, you like that? You want it now, baby?* I murmur, my tits pressed hard, my nipples flicking your back. You shove yourself down on my hand, it is such a fucking blessing to feel my fist pushing into you, your cunt wrapping around my hand perfect, and your thick plug swollen as I start bashing into it. I fuck you until both my forearms are sore, then my upper arms, then my lower back as I am heaving my whole body back and forth. I pump you, you arch up, boy body like a fish rising up, bellies slapping, my other hand slipping in your ass, finger reaching up and rubbing your asshole, then I push in and get all of you on me, until you scream jet spurt come like a boy spraying piss and gush onto my slip, my thighs, my belly. Push yourself down again and you spurt again, and again. Then throw my hand out of you saying, *Hold me can you just please hold me, I need a break* and I collapse there, feeling the dirt breeze lift the damp curls on the back of my neck, feeling you under me big. Close my eyes and everything is red.

After a while we wipe up, shake off, pull up this and that, then go tromping over the Williamsburg Bridge hand in hand. Home to the piss bottles and the thin junk-picked futon with the eggshell foam your last roommate stole from Fabricland. Curl up like alley kittens and crash out, fall asleep until the next day's warm soymilk and coffee.

It's ten years later, there's another war. Another city, another place crumbling, another neighbourhood "in transition." I don't think any place is safe from them, I've seen how they'll plumb every corner close enough to downtown by subway, every place that can become a renovated Victorian or a cool new loft space. A year later, you shot dope behind that wall, and it got the best of you. I mean literally, it took the best part of you, your bulk hollow behind that red and black Pendleton, you slipped and became someone I didn't recognize. And then I moved away so I could still recognize myself, so I could recognize myself more.

In my head I go back in time, I fuck you young again, from skinny to fat on $2.99 breakfasts, maybe Buddha's Delight on a good day. Behind that wall, brave enough, I fuck you until everything is red, until we come, until the wall breaks down, the cops turn and run, our apartment isn't bulldozed, *Patriot* doesn't get passed, we fight, not with each other, make a community garden outta a rubble-filled lot in that hood, we sleep on that eggshell foam. You don't die. I don't leave. We don't have to move on.

DR MALISS AND THE RISKY VENTURE

Miss Kitty Galore

"Bitch!"

Dr Marjory Maliss slammed the phone down on her large oak desk. She had already ended the call with the litigator but couldn't resist that old habit born of her early teen years, the reverberating noise that punctuated her rage. She stalked around her spacious office, high heels clicking out a furious Morse code on the tile floor. She cursed her publishing house, her editor, and her new team of lawyers that she had sent to hound them. She had spent the morning firing and re-hiring various consultants in a bid to get the upper hand in a recent set of lawsuits involving her new book and lecture series, *What Women Really Want: Emotional Ambush and Other Risky Ventures*. Out of the blue, she picked up the *feng shui* vase that doubled as a paperweight, a good luck present from a former secretary, and launched it at the far wall.

"Temper, temper." The curvaceous receptionist wagged her finger cheerfully from the open door. The tall blonde was dressed in a pale blue blouse and matching short skirt. "Shall I bring you my squeezy-stress toy, Dr Maliss? Or did you want me to close the door while you demolish your entire office?" She paused, then whispered, "You're scaring the clients again." She leaned against the door frame and crossed her arms below some particularly stunning cleavage.

The doctor's anger mushroomed. The last thing she needed was that dough-headed Barbie doll getting the moral high ground. "Close the door on your way out, Jennie."

"It's Jennifer," she said. The sound of pubescent injustice echoed faintly in her inflection. Jennifer flicked her blonde mane and closed the door behind her firmly, causing Dr Maliss to smirk.

It *was* difficult to remain annoyed once one's bad mood had spread to a previously unaffected individual. It was like giving away a head cold by sneezing on an unsuspecting victim. Dr Maliss removed her tailored black blazer and draped it on the back of her chair. She took a deep breath and rolled her shoulders vigorously. She lifted her archery set from its position of honour, the wall rack behind her impressive desk, and fired off a few singing arrows at the target hanging on her office door. The first two missed entirely, the third hit low. Finally, she exhaled slowly, checked her form, and took careful aim. She pulled the bowstring back taut, in line with her right ear, and let the arrow fly.

In that same fated instant, the doorknob turned. Jennifer's strained voice penetrated the room even as the weapon pierced her silk blouse. Both women stared in horrified silence at the slender shaft protruding from Jennifer's right shoulder.

"W-what is it?" Jennifer asked.

"My guess? Jones New York, sale rack at The Bay. At least two seasons old."

"What have you done?" she shrieked at her boss. A deep red stain was spreading through the fabric on the front of her blouse. She stared at Dr Maliss, eyes and mouth wide open.

"Shh," said the doctor. She guided Jennifer into the office and closed the door quietly. "We don't want to scare the clients, do we?"

Jennifer emitted a sound much like a squeak. She let herself be led to the couch and sat down. She was absolutely terrified and they both knew it.

"You know," Dr Maliss said carefully, "I *have* asked you several times to knock before entering my office."

Jennifer started to tremble.

"Now, let's not overreact," Dr Maliss continued. "That was a silly, preventable workplace accident. I'll have to find those WSIB forms. I know we have them somewhere." Dr Maliss yanked open the filing cabinet nearest her and began flipping through the vertical files. She kept talking but was somewhat distracted, searching for the human resources section. "How was I to know you'd burst in and interrupt me in the middle of a mood-clearing exercise?" she said. "A-ha!" She waved the file folder triumphantly, sat down beside Jennifer, and began to flip through the various papers.

"My shoulder, what about my shoulder?" Jennifer asked, tears welling up in her eyes and threatening to undo the many coats of mascara she was wearing. "Help me, Dr Maliss. It hurts." And so began the meandering salt water trail, tracked and preserved by inky black streaks spattering and trickling down Jennifer's powdered cheeks. When she looked down at the wound, she gasped. The bloodstain was enlarging its circle with every passing moment.

"Take it out," she hissed. "Please."

"Hmm. I don't think that's a very good idea," said Dr Maliss. She inspected the mess of blouse and blood. She wiped the lenses of her thick designer glasses and put them back on. "I don't think it's *too* deep. That's good, isn't it?"

Jennifer bit her lip. "Easy for you to say, you're not the one with an arrow in your shoulder." Her chin trembled as she spoke.

"Now, Jennifer," Dr Maliss said with mock surprise, "I told you it was an accident. There's no need to hold resentment. I'm only trying to help." She shrugged her non-disabled shoulder and spread her hands out, palms up, heart open. "Shall I get my medical bag and take a closer look?"

Jennifer nodded, but her eyes narrowed suspiciously.

The doctor stood up, towering over her receptionist. Her eyes bore down until the blonde girl had to look away. Jennifer sniffled and wiped her nose on the left sleeve of her ruined blouse. Then Dr Marjory Maliss smiled for real, for the first time all day. She retrieved the dusty bag from her closet and started to lay out various first aid instruments.

"Lie down, Jennie."

The girl did as she was told. She cradled her injured side and carefully leaned back onto the couch.

"Very good. Now sit up nice and tall."

Jennifer started to protest. "Why?"

"Because I said so." Then Dr Maliss snapped a clean white cloth in the air and barked, "Sit — up — now."

Jennifer awkwardly did as she was told, confused and fearful. She kept her mouth shut. The red stain covered her entire shoulder and was seeping down towards her tiny waist.

The scissors gleamed. Dr Maliss held the cold metal next to Jennifer's neck. "I have to remove that terrible blouse of yours," she said. She snipped and snipped. The doctor gently pulled away pieces of the soaking fabric and tossed them into a wastebasket. She cut around the arrow's shaft, around the puncture wound, so that only a small square of blouse remained. She began to tug on that piece, but Jennifer winced in pain. Dr Maliss dabbed Jennifer's bare skin with the towel. "You have lovely breasts," she said.

Jennifer looked up but didn't say a word.

"I really like your brassiere." She ran the scissors lightly across the top edge of the lace-embroidered, push-up, balconet-style black cups. Goosebumps rose on Jennifer's skin.

"Let me guess. Victoria's Secret, Glamour Collection, 2005. I'm right, aren't I?"

Jennifer raised a delicate eyebrow. "Advance promo sampler. Winter, 2006."

A muscle ticked in Dr Maliss's jaw. She continued snipping and, without blinking, severed the lacy strap in two.

Jennifer gasped. Her nostrils flared.

Dr Maliss set the scissors down on the glass coffee table and reached for the gauze. "It's been a while since I've dressed any wounds. Physical ones, at least." She began to wind and wrap layers of the soft cotton on either side of the wooden shaft. "On the count of three, Jennifer. One, two —"

"What's happening on —"

"Three!" Marjory pulled the arrow in a clean jerking motion, ripping it out from Jennifer's flesh.

Jennifer fainted.

When she came to, the strong smell of antiseptic was in the air. Dr Maliss had taped a thick gauze pad to the injured area and was pressing her large hand against it to stop the flow of blood. She was staring off into the distance, unaware that Jennifer was awake. Dr Maliss still looked severe, but not quite as intimidating as usual. Her jet black hair was tightly knotted in its perpetual dramatic bun, but she had removed her unattractive, thick glasses. Jennifer could see the fine lines that were starting to form around her eyes in spite of expensive spa visits and designer moisturizers. It made her seem more human, for once. She was a strangely handsome woman, elegant and terrifying, in a vaguely operatic way. In the several weeks since Jennifer had been hired, she had never seen the woman as quiet or still as in this moment.

Apart from this moment, Dr Maliss was, in all respects, a tornado of activity. Aside from her bustling career and the sudden semi-fame accrued from recent daytime television show appearances, she would hit the salon with ritualistic fervor prior to heading out for her notorious evenings of debauchery. Jennifer sometimes overheard heated conversations with both women and men whose hearts and genitals had been broken by the doctor. Jennifer spent a fair amount of time returning unwanted gifts, acknowledging exotic bouquets, fielding obsessive phone calls, and lying about the doctor's whereabouts when former suitors and lovelorn admirers came calling — not exactly what Jennifer had expected when the internationally renowned psychiatrist had hired her. The doctor was downright cruel.

Dr Maliss turned and caught the girl staring. She returned the look and pushed a bit harder on the gauze pad. Jennifer exhaled sharply.

"How are you feeling?" Dr Maliss asked quietly.

Jennifer bit her lip. "Will you please call my boyfriend to come pick me up?"

"Your boyfriend? Or the guy you fuck on your lunch break?" The doctor laughed as Jennifer's face darkened. "Next time, try taking a minute to lock the washroom door."

Jennifer pushed away from the doctor, lurched off the couch, and sputtered in disbelief.

"Don't worry, I won't tell on you. Who am I to intervene in riotous acts of passion? Certainly I'm not *that* much of a hypocrite." She walked towards Jennifer and rested one hand at the base of Jennifer's neck. Her long fingers drummed rhythmically at the top of Jennifer's spine, and traced circles around her left shoulder to release some tension. "How's that bandage feel on you?"

"Fine. I mean, it hurts, but —"

Dr Maliss pulled down the broken bra strap and peeled the material away from Jennifer's round breast. Without a word, she licked up Jennifer's tears and blood and the warm scent of her skin and set her large nipple to attention. Jennifer whimpered. The doctor backed her up onto the large desk. Dr Maliss unhooked the bra one-handed, drew the fabric away, and tossed it in a pile on top of the desk. Her mouth moved in for more delectable décollage. When Jennifer tried to speak, the doctor simply covered her mouth with kisses, soft and teasing, deep and biting.

Jennifer had already experienced one of the strangest days in her entire life. She had been pushed from one emotional extreme to another, been shot with an arrow, wounded and bandaged, and now seduced by her own employer. She decided to go with it. She relaxed her jaw and kissed back with no small amount of flirtation.

The doctor rested her warm hands on her receptionist's thighs, then without warning, violently pushed them apart as far as the skirt would allow. She insinuated her knuckles up against Jennifer's panties and pressed. With her other hand, she held firmly against Jennifer's lower back. Those fingers worked to undo the button and zipper of the skirt, and travelled down, hungry for bare skin. Both hands attacked Jennifer's panties simultaneously. Her right hand found Jennifer's surprised cunt; her left, the crevice of Jennifer's ass. Jennifer rocked back and forth slowly, enjoying a bit of both.

"Want to know the real reason I hired you?" Dr Maliss asked. She put three fingers in her own mouth and sucked them, wet them thoroughly, then slid them back between Jennifer's legs. She pressed on Jennifer's clit, swirled between her slick labia, pushed in deep, and pressed her fingers up and rocked slowly, steadily, adding pressure with the palm of her hand against the shaved mound. Jennifer's cunt squeezed back affectionately. Dr Maliss licked and sucked Jennifer's earlobe and nuzzled her neck, but carefully avoided the gauze padding and wound.

"I hired you so I could imagine fucking you every day of the week, not so I could watch you screw some college drop-out on your break," Dr Maliss whispered in Jennifer's ear. "I hired you so I could think about *this*." The doctor then found Jennifer's anus with an adventurous index finger.

"Oh," said Jennifer. She brought her feet up to the desk's edge, pushed onto her back, and lifted her hips in the air to better accommodate the doctor, who took the opportunity to remove Jennifer's pesky skirt.

"Look at Barbie now," whispered Dr Maliss. She pushed her left thumb into Jennifer's asshole and smiled when the girl moaned out loud. She continued to fuck her cunt with three strong fingers and occasionally licked at Jennifer's throbbing clit. "You're such a mess, aren't you? Your makeup is atrocious, your outfit is ruined, and you can't even use your right arm."

Jennifer lifted her legs up high and rested her shapely calves on the doctor's shoulders. She bit her lower lip and grunted as the thrusts became deeper, harder. She squeezed with her vaginal muscles and began to shoot a trail of hot juice out, over the doctor's hands, up in a graceful, golden arc, and into the doctor's shocked face. Dr Maliss tried to pull away, but was held captive by Jennifer's athletic cunt. She pulled her thumb out from the other orifice, but was berated by the receptionist: "Oh, no you don't!" Jennifer gripped the doctor's waist with her long legs, then used her high heels to jab at her. "I've put up with enough of your crap for weeks. The least you can do is fuck me properly, Doctor."

Dr Maliss, for once, was speechless. A sense of fierce competition and a hugely inflated ego fuelled her. She simply had to satisfy Jennifer. If the delivery guy could do it, so could she. Jennifer rearranged herself on the desk and bullied Dr Maliss into retrieving some latex gloves and lube from her purse, then dirty-talked her into some heavy fisting action. It took the better part of the afternoon, but when they were done, the doctor pushed up her sleeves, polished her glasses, and smiled widely at Jennifer, who was trying to catch her breath.

"I guess we worked out some of that earlier hostility," Dr Maliss said. She opened her top drawer and pulled out a marble ashtray, a packet of cigarettes, and a beautifully engraved lighter. She offered one to Jennifer, lit it, and did the same for herself.

"I don't know, Doctor," said Jennifer.

"Please, call me Marjory," she said indulgently.

"Marjory." Jennifer savoured the name for a moment. Then she said, "I expect an excellent reference and two months' pay directly deposited into my account, Marjory."

Marjory's cheek twitched, but she remained silent.

"And please don't forget those forms." She smiled and ground her cigarette out on the tile floor. She opened Marjory's closet, selected an expensive wool trench coat and a vibrant red scarf. She put them on and turned around slowly. "What do you think?"

Marjory kissed her cheek. "They suit you very well, Jennifer."

Jennifer paused dramatically, one hand on the doorknob. "Oh, and Marjory? I want that bra replaced."

The doctor smiled in spite of herself. "Of course. Please, close the door on your way out."

Jennifer stepped out and closed the door behind her. Rather gently, thought Marjory, with some regret. Rather too gently.

A FREE RIDE

Miss Cookie LaWhore

As a yellow cab pulled up to the curb, Dorothy turned to me — the car lights shining in her dark moony eyes — and asked, "Are you sure you don't mind?" We had called two cabs, since we were heading in opposite directions. She was a bio-girl, so I thought it safer for her to take the first, despite my micro-mini dress (100 percent pleather), messy black bob, dark lips, and goth-smeared eyes. We'd been at a party of lefties where she'd hoped a drag queen date would shake a few people up. Somehow, perhaps because I was still idealistic — meaning I was convinced drag could change the world one person at a time — I thought my outfit terribly clever and effective. But by the end of the night, while we were standing under the cold stars waiting for our rides, the suspicion that a vampy queen in a party of earnest politicos was a sorry marriage made me eager for home.

The cabbie switched off the lit sign on his car's roof. "You go first," I said, authoritatively. I gave her a kiss and she climbed in. We waved to each other as the cab pulled away.

Normally I'd take public transit. I'm a starving artist with a healthy dose of punk-rock in me, so I've been known to cut corners. "How'd you get here?" friends would ask at the bar, and I'd say, "Bus." By midnight, though, the streets are dangerous for hairy girls in tight dresses. I've had men threaten to kill me while I waited in something way too sexy for a bus stop. So during times like this, I step confidently to the curb and call out my three favourite letters of the alphabet: C, A, B.

When my cab pulled up, I climbed in the back seat, shivering, thankful for the heater. I was hoping my balls might drop back into place.

The cabbie said hello.

I replied with a simple hi and told him where I lived. Tired, I gazed out the window and watched the houses pass by slowly. We weren't travelling very fast. Before we'd reached the end of the first block, the driver asked, "Where were you tonight?"

"At a party," I said, "with friends."

"Fun party?" I could see his brown eyes just peak over the edge of the rear-view mirror, trying to get a look at me.

I said yes, then turned my head to the window to avoid his gaze. The houses were still passing slowly. Someone had Christmas lights on even though it was only early October.

He asked if I was going home. Thick hairs curled out from beneath his turban. The car smelled of leather and orange candy.

Yes, I answered again.

"Are you done for the night?" I looked at his eyes, steady in the mirror.

"Yah," I said, knowing I was repeating myself, "I'm going home."

He asked something then, in his slight accent, with his voice muffled. Something something blowjob. His eyes in the rear-view mirror stared into mine. The car crept even slower down the street.

"Pardon?" I asked, my stomach tightening with anticipation. I could gauge the intention of what he'd said, but I wanted to hear the request clearly so I could know how to answer him. I wanted to savour the sound of the request.

"One more blowjob?" he repeated.

"Maybe," I answered, getting hard so fast I was afraid I'd made stretch marks on my dick.

I realized his mistaken assumption. I was waiting on the street corner far from a gay bar, in drag, coming from a party with friends. He thought I was a prostitute. I decided not to tell him that I was a drag queen, not a tranny hooker, because that might spoil his mood.

"Where?" I asked.

"Your place?"

I waited, unsure how best to answer. I didn't want to go through the motions of parking the car, crossing the street, climbing the stairs, saying hello to my neighbours, unlocking the door, and digging his dick out of his pants. Left too long, any illicit idea turns stale.

"In the car," I said. My cock was pulsing against my panties. Each throb pushed it further up my abdomen.

"No car. Not safe to pull over."

"You can keep driving," I replied. My knees felt like they were tied together with loose thread.

He looked at me in the mirror again, then glanced out the side window, and looked back yet again. He shrugged a small yes, trying to seem indifferent, though his fingers tapped unconsciously on the steering wheel.

In a softer voice, I instructed him to pull over. He did. I adjusted my dick inside my panties to lay straight upwards, but still as I stepped out of the car, I was pointing skyward, ruining the line of my dress. I held a hand against my abdomen to mask the erection should anyone be looking out a living room window. Walking behind the car to the passenger side door, I wished I'd worn a longer coat.

Once inside, the orange candy smell was stronger in the front seat, though it wasn't on his breath. It came from somewhere nearby. I looked down at his pockets and could see his left hand cupping his lap.

I tapped the meter. "You should turn this off."

He made an odd, small grunt, then ran his fingers inside the flaps to his zipper. He pulled down his fly, slipped his hand into the lips of his pants and pulled out a squat brown cock. Immediately I wrapped my hand around it. Thick and moist to the touch, it felt warmer than my own skin. "Nice," I said, breathy.

He replied in a hushed slow voice, coaxing me: "Lick it ... lick it."

Soon, we were back on the road, my hand still on his dick. Just as we were turning onto a main street that cut diagonally through town on its way to my neighbourhood, I leaned over and breathed in the scent of his lap, sweet with sweat and a hint of sourness. He put his hand on the back of my neck and pushed me closer to his cock. I slid my mouth down the shaft, licking to the base and then back up again. I flicked his head with my tongue, quickly, a half dozen times.

As soon as I opened my mouth, he thrust upward, pushing his foot harder on the pedal by accident. The car raced ahead, engine revving, until he settled his ass back in the seat. I bobbed slowly on his dick, savouring it, cleaning it, and leaving my own perfume in the air. Again, he placed his hand on the back of my neck, encouraging me to go faster. I complied, loving his eagerness. I sucked him deep until my nose touched his groin, then slid my head to the side and took him a half-inch deeper still. Twisting at the neck on each retreat, I corkscrewed my mouth around his dick while moving my tongue in a variety of directions, sucking and licking at the same time.

His pants were loose enough that with the zipper undone, they stretched wide enough I could see his balls too. He wasn't wearing underwear. I wrapped his balls in my right hand and continued to suck him slowly and firmly.

He groaned. His hand was warm on my neck. Already I could taste the tinny sweetness of precum. As the cab rolled to a stop at a light, he said, "Up, up."

I gave him one last tight slurp and righted myself. There were cars on either side of us, but I didn't look at the drivers. I hoped someone noticed me in his lap, even though I didn't want to know who. A cop car passed through the intersection in front of us. I glanced at the cabbie from the corner of my eye. He was masturbating himself slowly.

The light was a long one. My cock pulsed with anticipation, hungry to get back in his lap.

As soon as the light turned green, he bolted ahead with a good press on the gas.

"More," he said, raising his arm above his shoulder to make his dick accessible. I crept in under his arm, which he then lowered onto me, and wrapped my fingers around him again. He sighed the instant I touched him.

"You like that?" I asked. He didn't answer. I repeated myself, determined to hear him say it.

"You suck it," he said, which was as much of a "yes" as I wanted.

I swallowed him down to the base again, holding my mouth there. My tongue wiggled back and forth across the base of his dick and his balls. He bucked again in his seat. The car lurched. I sucked him for a good few minutes and then jerked him off with my hand as I took his balls in my mouth. They were salty and rich, small enough to take both in at once. I rolled them over each other, bathing them with my tongue. He groaned, squeezing my shoulder for support. *I bet his wife doesn't do this for him,*

I thought. I felt pleased with myself. His driving felt reckless. I could feel the steering wheel press against my shoulder.

I moaned, letting it ripple through his ball sac. My mouth was full of him, wet, as I chewed a little, tugging his balls away from his body. He steered us around a corner; I was a few blocks from my building. Diving back on his dick, I turned up the speed, bobbing like mad, twisting more at the neck and grabbing his dick at the base. He groaned and pushed my head down harder, face-fucking me as best as he could with a foot on the gas. His breathing went staccato, his hand held me in place, and hot cum shot down my throat. His dick pulsed three, then four times, and he eased his grip on me. I sucked him a little more, slowly, driving the sensation home, to make him squirm with over-stimulation.

I sat upright just as we were pulling up on the other side of the street from my place. I adjusted my wig, then my dick, which was still straining heavenward. The cab's meter, I noticed, read $5.60. *That wasn't very bright*, I thought.

Once he put the car in park, he tried to collect the fare from me, as though he wasn't responsible for my tonsils feeling tender. I gave him a glare.

"Just give me five dollars," he said, shrugging again. He really sounded like he thought he was doing me a favour.

I picked my purse up off the seat and held it in my right hand. "I told you to turn the meter off."

"Just five dollars."

"Look," I said compassionately, but clearly, "a blowjob is fifty bucks. You're forty-five dollars up. I'm not paying you." With that, I stepped out of the car and shut the door with a flourish. By the time I wiggled my ass across the street — a parting gift — I'd forgotten him.

YES MEANS YES

May Lui

I'm alone in my apartment, the door unlocked. I'm slouching in my over-sized chair, reading. I don't hear the door open. I don't hear you come in, close the door behind you, and lock it. I don't see you until your shadow falls across my book. Startled, I look up, smiling. You look down at me, not smiling. Your eyes are hot and intense on mine. I start to say something painfully ordinary — "Hi," or "Do you want something to drink?" — but before I can speak, you shake your head at me.

You take my book from me, throw it to the floor. You lean down over me, pinning my shoulders back against the chair, your strong hands holding me in place. You kiss me hard, teeth nibbling and biting my lips, tongue invading my mouth. You kiss as if forever is tomorrow, until my body becomes soft, relaxed, desire slowly surfacing. My skin is alive from your touch. I'm completely aroused. Small moans surface at the back of my throat.

You kiss, bite, and nibble your way down my neck, collarbone, shoulders, to the round tops of my breasts, which are bulging out of the sports bra I'm wearing as a top. You groan a bit in my ear. In between your hard breathing and low moaning, I can hear you whisper, "I want you so much. I'm going to fuck you so hard. I'm going to make you come for me." I throw my head back, my breath comes faster, harder. My skin is flushed and hot. *Yes,* I think, *Oh yes,* my thoughts getting lost on the way to turning words into speech.

Suddenly you stop, drag me to my feet, and, holding me tightly, you walk me backward to the nearest wall, where you slam me hard against it, and continue your attack on my senses, your rough seduction. You grab both my wrists, one in each hand, and hold them down by my hips against the wall, as you bite and nibble at my breasts through my bra, swirling your tongue around my nipples. You drag one side of my bra down with your teeth, exposing my nipple, hard and aching, and lick and suck it, teasing and pulling and scraping your teeth around and along it. I struggle to free my hands, and I feel the force of your grip holding me.

You then straighten up, push my arms above my head and, dragging my bra off with one hand, you use it to hold my wrists together. Your other hand moves down my body, over my thin satin panties, while your mouth finds mine again, kissing me. Your fingers slide under the elastic waistband. You pull my panties down roughly, then rip them off me, and finally, finally your hand finds me, wet, dripping, wanting you.

My arms struggle against you. I need to find and feel the resistance of your strength, as you feel mine. I feel your thumb against my throbbing clit, one finger dipping into my wet cunt, one finger resting just outside my asshole.

"Yes," I whisper, spreading my legs open. "Yes," and with that word I give you my desire, my passion, my surrender. Yes.

You start to fuck me, slowly, grinding your body against mine as your fingers each start to press more deeply, turning, swirling, tickling. I press my hips towards you, moaning low in my throat. I'm wetter now, hotter. You're still kissing my swollen mouth, running your tongue along my lips, inside my mouth, biting my upper and lower lip, possessing me, for this moment.

I feel my first orgasm building, my breath catches, gasps out, my head whips back against the wall. It overtakes me and I come, wave over wave, again and again. You're holding me, watching me lose control. As my first orgasm subsides, my breath slows, I feel sweat on my face, between my breasts. I forget my hands are still trapped and try to reach for you, to stroke your face.

You shift to kneel in front of me, bringing my bound hands down to rest on my belly, holding them there with one hand. The fingers of your other hand spread my lips as you lean in to lick and tease the edge of my clit, just a few flicks, then you blow gently all over my clit, inner and outer lips, flick again with your tongue, over and over, slow torturous pleasure as my wetness drips slowly down my leg. Then, holding my hips firmly, you nibble and lick and probe everywhere, your tongue, teeth, lips going all around my clit, dipping into the opening of my aching cunt, wet still, so wet. I begin to pant, I close my eyes, lean back against the wall, as one leg moves up and flops open, wrapping around your back. I'm moaning louder, gasping, whimpering, "I'm so close, so close. Yes. Oh, yes." Your lips and tongue are on fire, never stopping, quickening their rhythm. You feel I am approaching the edge and, devouring me, take me over. I come, shuddering, moaning, groaning, feeling spasms of pleasure and desire. My clit, my cunt, waves rolling over me, over, then gradually slowing. My breath calms again.

You then stand up and, guiding me around the shoulders with one hand, holding my trapped arms with the other, you slowly back me into my bedroom, through darkness, onto my bed, where you tie down my arms, strap on your cock, and lay down beside me. I'm quivering again with anticipation, with hot desire, with wanting you. You touch me slowly with your fingertips, up and down my body, over my skin, circling my nipples, pinching them, then around the edges of my mouth, teasing me, letting me barely lick your fingers, barely taste them, before running them back down my body and tangling them in the hair of my pussy, wet and glistening. I arch my hips towards you, moaning again, and you slowly move your hand away.

"What do you want?" you whisper in my ear. "Tell me." Your fingertips begin their sweet, taunting journey again, over my body. "Tell me, slowly." I try to speak, lick my lips, swallow, try again. "I want you...."

"Yes?"

"... to ..."

"To what?"

"... take me, fuck me, don't stop touching me. Oh yes, yes."

You ease yourself between my legs, barely touching my cunt with the tip of your cock. Teasing me, circling, getting your tip wet and covered with me, my juice, my wetness. You slowly plunge in, fucking me the way I like to begin — in a bit, stop, out, in a bit more. All while the fingers of one hand are stroking my clit, so gently, so softly, until you're thrusting all the way inside me, grinding against my clit as you fuck me deep, again, again.

Again. I feel another orgasm build, release, subside. Another. Another. You fuck me senseless, you fuck me tenderly, you fuck me until I know nothing. I only feel. I only feel you, your mouth, my arms still tied, your tongue, your cock, your fingers. Yes.

FISHERMAN

Nalo Hopkinson

[An extended version of this story was originally published in the author's short story collection, Skin Folk.*]*

"You work as what; a fisherman?"

I nearly jump clean out my skin at the sound of she voice, tough like sugar cane when you done chew the fibres dry. "Fisherm ..." I stutter.

She sweet like cane too? Shame make me fling the thought 'way from me. Lord Jesus, is what make me come here any atall? I turn away from the window, from the pure wonder of watching through one big piece of clear glass at the hibiscus bush outside. Only Boysie house in the village have a glass window, and it have a crack running crossways through it. The rest of we have wooden jalousie shutters. I look back at she proud, round face with the plucked brows and the lipstick red on she plump lips. The words fall out from my mouth: "I ... I stink of fish, don't it?"

A smile spread on she beautiful brown face, like when you draw your finger through molasses on a plate. "Sit down nuh, doux-doux, you in your nice clean press white shirt? I glad you dress up to come and see me."

"All right." I siddown right to the edge of the chair with my hands in my lap, not holding the chair arms. I frighten for leave even a sniff of fish on the expensive tapestry. Everything in this cathouse worth more than me. I frighten for touch anything, least of all the glory of the woman standing in front of me now, bubbies and hips pushing out of she dress, forcing the cloth to shape like the roundness of she. The women where I living all look like what them does do: market woman, shave ice seller, baby mother. But she look like a picture in a magazine. Is silk that she wearing? How I to know, I who only make for wear crocus bag shirt and daddy old dungarees?

She move little closer, till she nearly touching my knees. From outside in the parlour I hearing two-three of the boys and them laughing over shots of red rum and talking with some of the whores that ain't working for the moment. I hear Lennie voice, and Two-Tone, though I can't really make out what them saying. Them done already? I draw back little more on the fancy chair.

The woman frown at me as if to say, *who you is any atall?* The look on she face put me in mind of when you does pull up your line out of the water sometimes to find a ugly fish gasping on the end of it, and instead of a fin, it have a small hand with three boneless fingers where no hand supposed to grow. She say, "You have a fainty smell of the sea hanging round you, is all, like this sea-shell here."

She lean over and pick up a big conch shell from she windowsill. It clean and pink on the inside with pointy brown parts jooking out on the outside.

She wearing a perfume I can't even describe, my head too full up with confusion. Something like how Granny did smell that time when I was small and Daddy take me to visit she in town. Granny did smell all baby powder and coconut grater-cake. Something like the ladies-of-the-night flowers too, that does bloom in my garden.

I slide back little more again in the chair, but she only move closer. "Here," she say, putting the shell to my nose. "Smell."

I sniff. Is the smell I smell every living day Papa God bring, when I baking my behind out on the boat in the sun hot and callousing up my hands pulling in the net next to the rest of the fishermen and them. I ain't know what to say to she, so I make a noise like, "Mmm...."

"Don't that nice?" She laugh a little bit, siddown in my lap, all warm, covering both my legs, the solid, sure weight and the perfume of she.

My heart start to fire *budupbudup* in my chest.

She say, "Don't that just get all up inside your nose and make you think of the blue waves dancing, and the little red crabs running sideways and waving they big gundy claw at you, and that green green frilly seaweed that look like it would taste fresh like lettuce in your mouth? Don't that smell make your mind run on the sea?"

"It make my mind run on work," I tell she.

She smile little bit. She put the shell back. "Work done for tonight," she tell me. "Now is time to play." She smoky laugh come in cracked and full up of holes. She voice put me in mind of the big rusty bell down by the beach what we does ring when we pull in the catch to let the women and them know them could come and buy fish. Through them holes in the bell you could hear the sea waves crashing on the beach. Sometimes I does feel to ring the bell just for so, just to hear the tongue of the clapper shout, "Fish, fish!" in it bright, break-up voice, but I have more sense than to make the village women mad at me.

She chest brush my arm as she lean over. She start to undo my shirt buttons. *No, not the shirt.* I take she hands and hold them in my own, hold her soft hands in my two hard own that smell like dead fish and fish scale and fish entrails.

The madam smile and run a warm, soft finger over my lips. I woulda push she off me right then and run go home. In fact I make to do it, but she pick up she two feet from off the floor and is then I get to feel the full weight and solidness of she.

"You go throw me off onto the hard ground, then?" she say with a flirty smile in she voice.

One time, five fifty-pound sack of chicken feed tumble from Boysie truck and land on me; two-hundred-fifty pounds drop me baps to the ground. Boysie had was to come and pull me out. Is heavy same way so she feel in my lap, grounding me. This woman wasn't going nowhere she ain't want to go.

"I ..." I start to reply, and she lean she face in close to mine, frowning at me the whole while like if I is a grouper with a freak hand. She put she two lips on my own. I frighten I frighten I frighten so till my breath catch like fish bone in my throat. Warm and soft she mouth feel against mine, so soft. My mouth was little bit open. I ain't know if to close it, if to back back, if to laugh. I ain't know this thing that people does do, I never do it before. The sea bear Daddy away before he could tell me about it.

She breath come in between my lips. Papa God, why nobody ever tell me you could taste the spice and warmth of somebody breath and never want to draw your face away again? Something warm and wet touch inside my lips and pull away, like a wave on a beach. She tongue! Nasty! I jerk my head, but she have it holding between she two hands, soft hands with the strength of fishing net. I feel the slip slip slip of she tongue again. She must be know what she doing. I let myself taste, and I realize it ain't so nasty in truth, just hot and wet with the life of she. My own tongue reach out, trembling, and tip to twiny conch tip touch she own. She mouth water and mine mingle. It have a tear in the corner of one of my eyes, I feel it twinkling there. I hear a small sound start from the back of my throat. When she move she face away from me, I nearly beg she not to stop.

She grin at me. My breath only coming in little sips, I feeling feverish, and what happening down between my legs I ain't even want to think about. I strong. I could move my head away, even though she still holding it. But I don't want to be rude. I cast my eyes down instead and find myself staring at the two fat bubbies spilling out of she dress, round and full like the hops bread you does eat with shark, but brown, skin-dark brown.

I pull my eyes up into she face again. "Listen to me now," she say, "I do that because I feel to. If you want to kiss the other women so you must ask permission first. Else them might box you two lick and scream for Jackobennie. You understand me?"

Jackobennie is the man who let me in the door of this cathouse, smirking at me like he know all my secrets. Jackobennie have a chest a bull would give he life to own and a right arm to make a leg of ham jealous. I don't want to cross Jackobennie atall atall.

"You understand me?" she ask again.

Daddy always used to say my mouth would get me in trouble. I open it to answer she yes, and what the rascal mouth say but, "No, I ain't understand. Why I could lick inside your mouth like that but not them own? I could pay."

She laugh that belly laugh till I think my thighs go break from the shaking. "Oh sweetness, I believe a treasure come in my door this day, a jewel beyond price."

"Don't laugh at me." If is one thing I can't brook, is nobody laughing at me. The fishermen did never want me to be one of them. I had was to show up at the boat every blessed morning and listen to the nasty things them was saying about me. Had to work beside people who would spit just to look on me. Till them come to realise I could do the work too.

I hear enough mockery, get enough mako make 'pon me to last all my days.

She look right in my eyes, right on through to my soul. She nod. "I would never laugh after you, my brave one, to waltz in here in your fisherman clothes."

Is only the fisherman she could see? "No, is not my work clothes I wearing. Is my good pair of pants and my nice brown shoes."

"And you even shine the shoes and all. And press a crease into the pants. I see that. I does notice when people dress up for me. And Jackobennie tell me you bring more than enough money. That nice, sweetness. I realize is your first time here. Is only the rules of my house I telling you; whatever you want to do, you must ask the girls and they first. And them have the right to refuse."

After I don't even know what to ask! Pastor would call it the sin of pride, to waltz in the place thinking my money could stand in place of good manners. "I sorry, Missis; I ain't know."

Surprise flare on she face. She draw back little bit to look at me good. "And like you really sorry, too. Yes, you is a treasure, all right. No need to be sorry, darling. You ain't do nothing wrong."

The ladies-of-the-night scent of she going all up inside my nostrils. The other men and they does laugh after me that I have a flower bush growing beside the pigeon peas and the tomatoes, so womanish, but I like to cut the flowers and put inside the house to brighten up the place with their softness and sweet smell. I have a blue glass bottle that I find wash up on the shore one day. The sand had scour it so it wasn't shining like glass no more. From the licking of the sea and the scrape of the sand, it had a texture under my fingertips like stone. I like that. I does put the flowers in it and put them on my table, the one what Daddy help me make.

"So, why you never come with the other fishermen? When you pull up to the dock all by yourself in that little dinghy, I get suspicious one time. I never see you before."

All the while she talking, and me mesmerized by she serious brown eyes, and too much to feel and think about at once, I never realize she did sliding she hand down inside my blouse, down until she fingers and thumb slide round one of my bubbies and feel the weight of it. Jesus Lord, she go call Jackobennie now! I make to jump up again, terror making me stronger, but this time she look at me with kindness. It make me weak. "Big strong woman," she whisper.

She know! All this time, she know? I couldn't move from that chair, even if Papa God heself was to come down to earth and command me. I just sitting there, weak and trembling, while she undo the shirt slow, one button at a time, drag it out of my pants, and lay my bubbies bare to the open air. The nipples crinkle up one time and I shame I shame. Nothing to do but sit there, exposed and trembling like conch when you drag it out of the shell to die.

I squinch my eyes closed tight, but feel a hot tear escape from under my eyelid and track down my face. So long nobody ain't see me cry. I feel to dead. I wait to hear the scorn from she dry-ashes voice.

"Sweetheart?" Gentle hands closing back my shirt, but not drawing away; resting warm on the fat shameful weight of my bubbies. "Mister Fisherman?"

Yes. Is that I is. A fisherman. I draw in the breath I been keeping out, a long, shuddery one. She hands rise and fall with my chest. I open my eyes, but I can't stand to look in she face. I away gaze out the window, past the clean pink shell to the blue wall of the sea far away. What make me leave my home this day any at all, eh?

"Look at me, nuh? What you name?"

I dash way the tear with the back of my hand, sniff back the snot. "K.C."

"Casey?"

"Letter K, letter C. For 'Kelly Carol': K.C. I sorry I take up your time, Missis. You want me to go?" I chance a quick glance at her. She get that weighing and measuring look again. The warmth of she hands through my shirt feeling nice. Can't think 'bout that.

"Why you come here in the first place, K.C.?"

I tilt my head away from her, look down at my shoes, my nice shine shoes. Oh God, how to explain? "Is just I ... look, I not make for this, I not a ... I did only want some company, the way the other men and they does talk about all the time. All blessed week we pulling on the nets together, all of we. And some of the men does even treat me like one of them, you know? A fisherman, doing my job. Then Saturday nights after we go to market them does leave me and come here, even Lennie, and I hear next day how sweet allyou is, all of allyou in this cathouse. Every week it happen so and every Saturday night I stay home in my wattle and daub hut and watch at the kerosene lamp burning till is time to go to bed. Nobody but me. But I catch plenty fish and sell in the market today, I had enough money, and after them all come here I follow them in one of Lennie small boats. I just figure is time, my turn now ... but I will go away. I don't belong here." My heart feeling heavy in my chest. I sit and wait for she to banish me.

She laugh like a dolphin leaping. "K.C., you don't have to go nowhere. Look at me, nuh?"

The short distance I had was to drag my eyes from the window to she face was like I going to dead, like somebody dragging a sharp knife along the belly of a fish that twisting in your hands. My two eyes and she own make four, and I feel my belly bottom drop out same way so that fish guts would tumble like rope from it body.

She start to count off on she fingers: "You come in clean clothes; you bathe too, I could smell the carbolic soap on your skin; you not too drunk to have sense; you come prepared to pay; you have manners. Now tell me; why I would turn away such a ideal customer?"

"I ... because I ..."

"You ever fuck before?"

"No!" My face burning up for shame. I hear the word plenty time. I see dogs doing it in the road. I not sure what it have to do with me. But I want to find out.

She give me one mischievous grin. "Well, doux-doux, is your lucky night tonight; you going to learn from the mistress of this house!"

Oh God.

Softly she say, "You go let me touch you, K.C.? Mister fisherman?"

My heart flapping in my chest like a mullet on a jetty. She must be can feel it jumping under she hands. I whisper, "Yes, please."

And next thing I know, my shirt get drag open all the way. She say, "Take it off, nuh? I want to see the muscles in your arms."

My arms? I busy feeling shamed, 'fraid for she to watch at my bubbies — nobody see them all these years — but is my arms she want to see? For the first time this night, I crack one little smile. I pull off the shirt, stand there holding it careful by the collar so it wouldn't get rampfle. She step in closer and squeeze my one arm, and when she look at me, the look make something in my crotch jump again. Is a look of somebody who want something. My smile freeze. I ain't know what to do with my face. My eyes start to drop to the floor again. But she put she hand under my chin. "Watch at me in my eyes, K.C.; like man does look at woman."

My blasted tongue run away with me again. "And what it have to look at? You seeing more of me than I seeing of you."

A grin that could swallow a house. "True. Help me fix that then, nuh?" And she present me with she back, one hand cock-up on she hip. "Undo my dress for me, please?"

She had comb she hair up onto her head with a sweep and a frill like wedding cake icing, only black. The purple silk of the gown come down low on she back so I could see all that brown skin, smelling like sweet flowers. The fancy dress-back fasten with one set of hook and eye and button and bow. I tall, nearly tall like Two-Tone, but this woman little bit taller than me, even. I reach up to the top of she dress-back. I manage to undo three button and a hook before a button just pop off in my hand. "Fuck, man, I can't manage these fancy things; I ain't make for them. Missis, I done bust up your dress, I sorry."

She feel behind she, run one long brown finger over the place where the button tear from. Quicker than my eyes could follow, she undo the dress the rest of the way. I see she big round bamsie naked and smooth under there, but she step away and turn to face me before I could see enough. "Give me the button."

I hand it to she. She laugh little bit and drop it down between she bubbies. "Oh, look what I gone and do. Come and find it for me, nuh?"

Is like somebody nail my two foot-them to the floor. I couldn't move. I feel like my head going to bust apart. I just watch at she. She step so close to me I could smell she breath warm on my lips. I want to taste that breath again. She whisper, "Find my button for me, K.C."

I don't know when my hands reach on she shoulders. Is like I watching a picture film of me sliding my hands down that soft skin to the opening of the dress, moving my hands in and taking she two tot-tots in each hand. They big and heavy, would be about three pound each on the scale. If I was to price this lady pound for pound, I could never afford she. I move my hand in to the warm, damp place in between she bubbies. The flower smell rising warm off she. My fingers only trembling, trembling, but I pick out the button. I give it back. She stand there, watching in my eyes. Is when I see she smile that I realize I put the fingers that reach the button in my mouth. She taste salt and smell sweet. She push the dress off one shoulder, then the next one. It land on she hips and catch there. Can't go no further past the swelling of she belly and bamsie without help. And me, I only watching at the full and swing and round of she bubbies and is like my tongue swell up and my whole body it hot it hot it hot like fire.

"You like me?" she say.

"I ... I think so."

"Help me take off my dress the rest of the way?"

She telling me I could touch she. My mother was the last somebody what make me touch their body, when I was helping Daddy look after she before she dead. Mummy was wasting away them times there. She skin was dry and crackly like the brown paper we does wrap the fish in. But this skin on this lady belly and hips put me in mind of that time Daddy take me to visit my granny in the town; how Granny put me on she knee and give me cocoa-tea to drink that she make by grating the cocoa and nutmeg into the hot water; how Granny did wearing a brown velvet dress and I never touch velvet, before neither since, and I just sit there so on Granny knee, running my thumb across a little piece of she sleeve over and over again, drinking hot cocoa-tea with plenty condensed milk. This woman skin under my hands put me in mind of that somehow, of velvet and hot cocoa with thick, sweet condensed milk and the delicious fat floating on top. As I pass my hands over this woman hips to draw down the dress the rest of the way, I feel to just stop there and do that all evening, to just touch she flesh over and over again like a piece of brown velvet.

Then she make a kind of little wiggle and the dress drop right down on the ground and is like I get transfix. My two eye-them get full up of beauty and if God did strike me dead right there, I woulda die happy.

She only smiling, smiling. "Like you like what you see, eh, Fisherman?"

"Yes, ma'am."

She step out the dress and go over to the bed. She lie back on it and I mark how she bubbies roll to either side when she do so. Today I bring back two fat, round pumpkin from the market, rolling around in my basket. The soup from those pumpkins going to be nice. I taste the salt on my lips still from when I touch she bubbies and lick my fingers after.

She say, "Come over here, K.C."

I go and sit on the edge of the bed, not too close. And now I shame again, for it have a white crochet spread on the bed, and white pillow cases on the pillows and them, with some yellow and pink embroidery edging the pillowcases. I can't get my fisherman stink all over this lady nice bed!

"Take off your shoes and your pants, K.C."

So I do that, giving thanks that I could turn my back on she and not see she watching when I get naked.

"The underwears too."

I drag off my underpants, the one good ones with no stain. I fold them up small small and put them at the foot of the bed. I leave my hand on them. They still warm from my body.

I feel to never leave that warmth.

"Come into bed with me."

So then I had was to turn around to climb on the bed. I feel so big and boobaloops and clumsy. I roll back the bedspread, careful and sit down on the sheet. I pull my knees up to my chest. I watch at she feet. Pretty feet. No callous, though.

She rise up in the bed, sit facing me. She ease the crochet bedspread out from under she body and roll it all the way down to the end of the bed. What she go do now? I nearly perishing for fright. "Lie back, K.C."

So I do that, stiff like one piece of plank. She lean over me, she chest hanging nearly in my face. If she come down any lower, how I go breathe? She start passing she hands over my two shoulders, side to side. Big, warm hands. Big like mine. All these years, is this my skin been hungry for. I feel my whole body getting warm, melting into the soft bed. I close my eyes.

"Nice?" she ask.

"Mm-hmm."

She hands pass side to side, side to side, so hot and nice on my skin. And then the hands go under my bubbies, weighing. I jump and my eyes start open, but the look on she face ain't telling me nothing. I turn a piece of board again, just lying there. She run she thumbs over my nipples and

I swear I feel it right down to my crotch. Is so I does do myself nights when the skin hunger get too bad, but Jesus God how it powerful when somebody else do it for you! My breath coming hard, making little sounds. Can't make she see, can't make she hear. I go to push she hands away.

"Is all right, K.C. Nothing for shame. Relax, nuh?"

"I doing it right?"

"When it feeling good, you doing it right."

I must be doing it plenty right, then. I put my head on the pillow again. She start to squeeze my bubbies, to pull and tug at them. I ain't know how much time past, I just get lost in what she hands doing. The little noises I making coming louder now.

I wonder if Lennie could hear me, and Two-Tone, but I decide I ain't care.

The woman hands on my belly now, massaging the big swell of it. Between my legs my blood only beating, beating. I want ... no, I ain't want that. How anybody could want that? But when she push my legs apart, when that big, warm hand cover my whole pum-pum and squeeze, I swear it try to leap into she hands. She push apart my legs little more, spread my pum-pum lips open. Oy-oy-oy I shame, but I couldn't stand to stop she. She press on that place, the place between my legs I find to rub so long ago. I forget how to breathe. "Look your little parson's nose there," she giggle. She take she hand away and I nearly beg she to put it back. She lick she fingers. She must be did watching my face, how it get disgust, for she say, "You never taste yourself?"

"Yes." My voice come out small.

"Well, then." She put the fingers back. Oh, God, the wetness she bring on she fingers just sliding and sliding on the button. And she rub and she rub and little more I thrashing round on the bed till she had was to lie over me with all she weight to make me keep still, make me stay open under she fingers and something coming from deep inside me it buzzing buzzing buzzing from way inside my body like I don't know what but it coming and I can't stop it, don't want to stop it and I barely hear myself and the noises I making and then it hit me like lightning and it ride me like a storm and I shout something, I ain't know what, and inside my pum-pum squeezing so hard and nice. I only sweating and trembling when the something drop me back on the bed. "Fuck."

"Exactly." She laugh, move off me. "You have a mouth like a fisherman, too."

Sweat drenching me, salt drying on my skin. My belly feeling all fluttery inside. I couldn't look at she. One time long long ago, one night time in my bed, I touch myself long time like she just touch me and I get a feeling little bit like she just give me, but it frighten me. I thought I was deading. I thought is because is nastiness I was doing. I pull my hand away, and the feeling stop. And though I figure out afterwards that I wasn't go dead, though I do that thing between my legs plenty times since and it feel nice, I never manage after that to make the feeling come back so strong again. "What we go do now?" I ask she.

"How you know we ain't finish, K.C.?"

I peek over my bubbies and belly at she. She sitting in between my legs like if it ain't have nothing wrong with that. She two massive legs pinning my own big ones down, brown on brown. I see she cocoa pod pum-pum, spread open pink and glistening, going to brown at the edges. Lord, what a thing. "I ain't feel finish yet, I feel like it have more."

She give me that rapscallion smile. "Oh yes, it could have plenty more."

She start to stroke my button again, gentle. I glad for that, for it feeling tender. Nice, though. I ain't really get surprised when she push a finger inside my pum-pum. Then another one. I do that myself, plenty times. I thought is only me do that. Me and my nastiness. I start to relax back on she fine white bedspread again, but all of a sudden I sitting up and pulling she hands away. "No. Stop."

She stop one time. "You don't like it?"

"I … I don't know." Then I bust out with, "I just feel … I not a glove you does wear for you to go inside me like that."

She just stroke my thighs, with a look on she face like she thinking. "All right then. Let we try something else."

Just like that? "Is all right?"

"Yes, K.C. Everybody different. You must tell me what you like and don't like. Move over so I could lie down."

I make room for she. She lie down on she back with one knee bend. "Touch me like I touch you."

Lord, but this thing hard to do. The way the boys and them talk, I did think it would be easy; just pay the woman and she fix you up.

I do she like she do me. I massage she shoulders, I play with she bubbies. So strange. Like touching my own, almost.

"Pull them."

I ain't know what she mean. She put she nipples between my fingers.

"Pull."

I tug little bit.

"Harder."

So I 'buse up she breasts for she. It look like she good and like it, though. She breathing coming in heavy. It make me feel good. Powerful. I knead she belly, and she spread open she legs for me. The pum-pum smell rise from she, like I used to smelling it on myself. I know that smell like my life. I start to relax. I rub she little button, but that ain't seem to sweet she so much. She only screwing up she face and twitching little bit when I touch she. I stop. "I not doing it right."

"It ain't have no right nor wrong, my fisherman. Just stroke it from the top to the bottom, very gentle."

Oho. Treat she tot-tots hard on top, she pum-pum soft down below. I could do that. I make the touch light, so light. In two-twos she start to say, "Mm," and "Ah," quiet-quiet like the first soft breeze of morning. I look at she face. She head only rolling from side to side, she eyes shut tight. She nipples crinkle up and jooking out. I feel if to kiss them. I wonder if I could do that? She belly shuddering. I think she liking it.

Something wetting my hand, down there where I stroking she. I look down. She pum-pum getting wet and warm and sticky. The salt and sweat smell rising up from she stronger. Now what to do? I ain't know what to do.

Do me like I do you, that is what she tell me. Maybe she don't mind being a glove. So I slip one finger inside the pum-pum. She kinda give a little squeak. It hot in there, and slippery. It only squeezing and squeezing my finger, tight. "Like this, missis?"

"Oh God, like that. Go in and out for me, nuh? No, no; only partway out. Yes, yes, K.C. like that."

I get a rhythm going; in, out, in.

"More fingers, K.C."

I could do that.

"More."

Four fingers inside she, fulling she up. She squeezing tight like a handshake now, and only getting wetter. And every push I push, my hand going in farther. I get lost in the warm wet and sucking and the little moans she making. She spreading she knees wider, tilting up she hips to get my fingers deeper in.

"Oh God, more."

More? Is only my thumb leave behind. I tuck it in close with the others and push that inside she too. She start to groan. I say, "I hurting you?" I start to pull my hand out.

"If you only take it out," she pant, "I swear I box you here tonight." She spread she two feet to either side of the bed, move she pum-pum up to meet me hand. "Push it, K.C. Push."

And is like a space opening up deep inside the poonani. Like it pulling. Like it hungry. I push a few little minutes more, with she groaning and rolling she head around. And next thing I know, is no lie, my whole hand pass through the tightest place inside she and slide into she poonani right up to the wrist! She groan, "Fuck me, K.C.!"

She hips bucking like anything. A strong woman this. I had was to brace myself, wrap one arm around she thigh and hold on tight. So close in there, I close my hand up into a fist. I pull back my hand partway, and push it in again. Pull back, push in. Pull back, push in. She start to bawl 'bout don't stop, fuck she, don't stop. I could do that. I hold on to she bucking body and I fuck she. Me, K.C. She only throwing sheself around steady on the bed. The way she head tossing, all she hair come loose from that pretty hairstyle. It twisting and knotting all over the two pillows. She belly shaking, she bubbies bouncing up and down, she thighs clamp onto me. And she bawling, bawling. This woman bawling like any baby here in this bed. I ride with she. I feel my own pum-pum getting warm, my button swelling and throbbing between my legs. I fuck she, I fuck she. She moan, she twist herself up. My shoulders burning from all the work I doing, but I just imagine I pulling in the net with the boys and them. Push your hand out, pull it back. Push it out, pull it back. Push, pull. I smelling pum-pum all 'round me and my sweat and she own.

All of a sudden, something deep inside she start to squeeze my hand fast-fast-fast like a pounding heart, so strong I frighten my hand going to sprain. She arch she back up right off the bed and she scream, "Oh GOD, I love a mannish woman!" And more too besides, but them wasn't exactly words.

Hmm. Mannish woman. I like better to be she fisherman. Now is not the time to tell she that, though.

The pounding inside she stop. She give a little sigh and reach down and grab my wrist to hold it quiet. She flop back down on the bed with that mischevious grin on she face again.

Somebody knock on the door. I jump and freeze. If I come out too fast, I might hurt she.

"Mary Anne? Everything all right?" Is a man voice.

She start to laugh. I could feel it right down in she belly.

"Jackobennie, you too fast. I with a customer. Leave we some privacy."

A deep chuckle roll into the room. "Sorry, girl. I ain't mean to disturb allyou; I gone."

I could hear the heavy weight of he footsteps as he walk away. Jackobennie is a giant of a man. My whole body start to feel cold one time. "You is Jackobennie woman?"

She lie back and close she eyes, squeeze my hand that jam up inside she. She smile. "Jackobennie is my right-hand man. He and me know one other since God was a little boy in short pants. Jackobennie does make sure me and the rest of the girls stay safe. Sometimes customers does act stupid. Don't fret your head about Jackobennie, K.C. You is a well-behaved customer."

I smile.

"Move the heel of your hand up and down for me, nuh? Ai! Gentle!"

I could do that. A sucking sound come from inside she poonani as she flesh move away little bit from my hand.

"Good. Now come out, slow."

My shoulder muscles burn as I pull out. My hand come back to me wet and wrinkly. I raise the hand to my mouth. It smell like she, like me. I taste it. I know that taste.

"Here." Mary Anne hand me a towel from out the bedside table. I wipe my hands.

My bubbies tingling.

Mary Anne sit up, she belly resting on she thighs like a calabash. When she grin at me again, I feel all warm inside.

"So, fisherman," she say, "what you think of your first time?"

"Nice. Strange. But nice."

"Like you. You going to come back and see me sometimes?"

"You want me to come back?"

"It have plenty more I could show you, sweetness."

My pum-pum feeling like a big, warm smile. I just done fuck somebody. The grin that break out on my face must be did brighter than the sun.

For that grin, she say, she kiss me again.

She count the money and tuck it into she bosom. She takes my hand. Nobody do that since I was a small child. We step outside the room and the sound of they wicked laughter singe the smile from my face.

POLLY

Zoe Whittall

1.

Understand me when I say I didn't plan anything. I never do. I had my hands almost inside his jeans. Finger trailing his lower back, making absent infinity signs. We just finished having breakfast after last call. Eggs eye sides-up. Nitrates and margarine rivers on cracked Formica. Our friends with eyebrows raised in suspicion at our occasional hands touching, the grazing of a cheek by a soft fingertip, a sweet glance. I'd watched him at the bar opening bottles of beer with his taut, muscled arms. Straddling him on the steps outside after our shift ended, it started raining fear. With each drop I felt stained. I pulled him on top of me, scraping my back against the cement. There were jewels on his tongue.

Nothing actually happened. Teasing. There are lines. The ones I negotiate with my girlfriend. They become actual lines of his jeans. When I sit on his lap, cradling his face in one hand, I will the other hand not to slip down, feel how hard his cock is, even though he doesn't really have one.

"Polly," he whispers, groaning. "Why do you have to be married?"

Declarations like this are interrupting my plan of a seamless affair. I get up to walk home. I trip on the head of a tulip lying next to an abandoned single dresser drawer in the middle of the sidewalk. I detour dizzily from the trajectory I outline. Rubbing my skinned knee, the lines of blood raising, all I can think about is rubbing his chest scars slowly with my finger tips. Something that will never happen.

When I get home I tell Sascha that I kissed the bartender.

"Was it good?"

"Sure. I mean, whatever."

"Well, at least it wasn't the DJ. I hate that fucking DJ."

We both turn away from each other, our heads on separate pillows, pretending to sleep.

2.

I'm lying across three girls' laps in the back of a cruiser, my short skirt rising up, visible in the side-view mirror. We used to crowd into taxis like this after work, promising a big tip if all of us could squeeze in the back seat. Sasha would sneak her hand under the bodies and tease me while I had to be quiet. Watch the upside-down city through the windows light up like a grainy, bright Super-8 film.

But this is a not a romantic segue, it is a bright white cop car, and Sasha sits limply under me. Turning to face us, the cop in the passenger seat tells her softly that if he had his way, all rapists would be shot. Sent to an island with all the AIDS faggots. We'll do what we can to make sure we find the guy who raped you and put him in jail. All four of us are quiet. Close our eyes, pretend he didn't say that. No use fighting. How does he not know we are all dykes? But dressed for work, all of us pass, even Sascha who's most comfortable in coveralls and combat boots, ties and dress shirts. I wish I were five and could ask him to play the sirens, spin the lights. When I am the first to pile out of the car, he grazes my nineteen-year-old ass, like it could be an accident, and gives me his card. "You're too pretty for a night like this," he whispers.

At the police station, Sascha tells the story over again. I heard it at the hospital, in both English and French. I heard it at Station 33. Now, at another station, she talks to the fourth detective. Apparently it takes a village to report a rape. They are going to look at computer photos of people who match his description. I hold her hand until I feel grafted to its sweaty underside. Scrolling screens of mug shots turn my stomach.

I tell her I need some air. Our two friends sit in the lobby on the hard wooden bench absently reading the pamphlets on bike safety.

I sit outside, watching the clock through the bank window across the street turn to 3:35 a.m. I try to light a smoke with matches from the club. They're cheap and crappy like everything from work.

Clean-cut cop boy is leaning against his car, looks up almost guiltily, like I've caught him slacking off. He'd almost be cute, hot even, if he wasn't the enemy. He approaches me with a lighter. "My partner went to get us some pizza. You hungry?"

"No."

I'm sitting on the stone steps. This isn't what I thought a police station was like in the middle of the night. I expected a bustle of criminals. Take-downs. It was quiet like a country night; the lights of the occasional passing taxi like a steady creak of crickets. I want Lenny from *Law and Order* instead. Fiction you can trust.

I open my legs a little, unstick my thighs in the humidity. Stare ahead. Right at his blue eyes, greased back hair. I look right into him. The intensity of my stare is the loudest thing on the street. We are in a stand-off, oddly intimate, eye contact for no reason. He is smiling, I try not to notice that he is getting hard. He is like a puppy, so unabashedly proud of his pure simplicity. I stare at the gun in his holster. He doesn't know what my face means.

"What's your name?"

"Polly." My alias comes out of my mouth quickly.

"I'm really sorry about your friend, Polly."

I hate it when people punctuate sentences with my name. It's an immediate indicator of want, of patronizing. And Sascha has never been my friend; my one and only true love, yes.

"You know, that's why I became a cop. You know? My dad was an asshole. He beat my mom up so bad. I want to make the world safer ..."

His mouth is moving. I stop listening.

"... for women...." His cock is straining against his uniform pants now, directly in front of me where I sit on the step. He isn't doing anything guys normally do to conceal it. He just stands there, brazen, as if his mouth is divorced from the lower half of his body. Impatience rises like an orgasm or a rotten meal inside me: desire and nausea are often mixed up in my body.

Just last night, I ran circles over my body, coming fast and hard to images of a boy-in-blue stroking against my ass, hard hand against my collar, sighing happily into a dream.

But the possibility of realizing this fantasy was not as exciting.

If this were a plot shift in a choose-your-own-misadventure story, it could happen like this, right now, on the steps of Station 21.

I could snap him up, bewildered, unzip him and grab at his purple-pink flesh. Suck furiously till my stomach hurts. *There*, I'd say, spitting on the step below. *There*, landing like a miniature ocean. The look of shock tattooed on his face would almost be worth it. I picture his cock laying limply, soft like a wet baby bird.

Instead I keep staring, bare legs cold against stone steps. Thinking a whirl of convoluted thoughts about power and men; these things I can't name but form burning pop rocks in my throat. And I have never lost a staring contest. He looks away first. Turns around, shifts uncomfortably in his uniform. Blushes.

I stand up, smirk, drop my smoke, and go back inside.

3.

Mystical is doing her floorshow to three Depeche Mode songs in a row. It's really quite sexy in a doomed sort of way. She calls me The Fetus and doesn't believe that I'm actually nineteen and not sixteen. "Wanna dance with The Fetus?" she says to men. "She's even younger than your daughter." And they get so uncomfortable that they don't know what to do when I grab their hands and lead them back to the VIP lounge.

I get a regular and take him back to the red couches, the cordoned-off area. He talks a lot and I nod. He wants to feel my tits, lick my nipples. He has white crusty bits in his moustache. Still, when I lean back, my hair grazing the floor and my hand absently circling my clit the way I normally would, my body betrays me by responding. He's talking about his latest farming catastrophe and I'm almost coming. I try to stop myself, mortified, but it might also feel good. Conflicted, I sit down on his lap and grab his hair with my free hand, muscles tense. I could snap his neck. I move my hand to my nipples instead and hear the song coming to an end, I stick my tits in his face so he doesn't notice the transition and will have to pay for another dance. "I can't afford another, Polly," he says. I stand up and snap my g-string back in place. Turn around without looking back and teeter up to the dressing room.

When I get home, Sascha has arranged all of our books in the house by colour and thrown out all the food. I'm really hungry and confused. I tell her that I want to take her to Niagara Falls for her birthday. If I make enough money this weekend, I can totally afford the heart-shaped tub, the casino package. Wouldn't that be fun? She shrugs. I fall asleep drunk on the couch listening to her chatter to the cat about a new system, a new her.

When I wake up dry-eyed and aching a few hours later, Sascha is sitting naked in the armchair in front of me, her long legs spread open, feet dangling over each plush red arm. Her long black hair is wet and curling around her neck. My first thought is, *Wow, she finally took a shower.* My second is, *She's stunning.*

She softly says, "Hey baby," as I get up from the couch, stretch out, staring. I want to take her photograph, wallpaper the room with this image over and over, how beautiful she looks. Pale skin against red chair and the inky lines of her hair.

I grab the Polaroid from the floor and snap her image. The flash makes her blink, startled, but her body remains still.

A girl like this, reclined, clean-shaven and posed, nipples hard and back arched, is something I see at work every day and find redundant. A too-familiar visual menu option. But at this moment I feel as though I understand the erotic trance bodies can cause. I put the Polaroid down, crawl across the room to her, speechless, unable to detach my gaze. I bury my head between her thighs. She twists her legs around me, clamping her ankles together like a twist-tie. I stay there all night, my knees bruising beautifully while her breath rises and falls too many times to count. Trying to bring her back to life.

4.

Jake, my new submissive sometimes-boyfriend, fastens the harness to my thighs, under my short red skirt. The pink cock dangles like a misplaced comma. It is my birthday present. I feel like I did at age ten when I really wanted a makeup set but got a sturdy ten-speed instead. "Makeup is a tool of the patriarchy," said my mother.

"Oh, that's so hot," says Jake.

I smile at him, trying to betray my disappointment and lack of enthusiasm. I had wanted new boots, the Nigella Lawson cookbook, lingerie, anything but a new pink appendage.

I step in front of the mirror. It sits like a clown nose, infantile and goofy, between my legs.

I fasten my high-heeled sandals, get a cold beer from the fridge, and sit down on the couch. Sascha is trying to stop herself from laughing, but can't.

"I don't know. I don't think I can go." I glance at the flyer for the fetish night as I open my beer. The flashy card features a girl dressed like a cat, a guy in a ball gag, and a list of DJ names I don't recognize.

Jake kneels in front of me. "I think I know how to change your mind," he says, then grabs at the cock, pulling it away from my skin, the harness digging into my legs. He sucks and licks, looking up at me for approval. I cannot fake it. I half-smile. Shrug.

"I feel like a dork," I offer.

He stands, disappointed. Reaches down to feel the dry proof of failure.

I stand in front of the mirror again. A complete detachment from what I see.

Sascha reaches into the harness and pulls the dildo out, sticking it between her lips like a cigar, giggling. She stuffs it down the front of her jeans, rubs it up and down, smiling. Her eyes say, *Later,* so that Jake doesn't see, because the carefully laid out polyamory rules dictate that Tuesdays are for him, and that's all he gets.

He's too busy drawing on his facial hair to notice our exchange. He makes me swoon when he turns toward us. Double swoon, a lucky girl.

DANCING QUEEN

Rachel Kramer Bussel

"I get turned on when I dance," she tells me with a twinkle in her eye as she sashays her way from my perch at the bar onto the dance floor, daring me to follow her. The hem of her red dress bounces around her thighs, and as she rocks her hips, her tight curls swing in reply. On the floor amid the other twirling, gyrating bodies, she immediately transforms herself into a better version of herself, completely at one with her body and the beat, oblivious to everything but the many ways she can move to the rhythm. The beat finds its way inside her and then works its way out. Meanwhile, my thoughts are less pure as I look at her pulsating body and imagine what I could do with it in a slightly different setting, making our own very private music.

In my purse, I'm holding the blindfold that has been there for the last three months. It was less an impulse purchase than one of those items you know you need, know you've been lacking something without it, know your life is incomplete unless you own it the moment you see it — the blindfold is a purchase that immediately yields results, immediately fills some void that you're stunned to realize you didn't know existed, makes its presence known throughout the day even when it's not in use. It's not so much a toy or an "aid" as a necessity, a vital part of my newfound fantasy life. It is plush and decadent, padded purple and black velvet, soft and delicate yet surprisingly sturdy. I've briefly submitted to its tenderness, telling myself I needed to see if it worked, though what I most long for is to see it wrapped around a lover's eyes, tenderly sinking them into a dense, delicious darkness from which there is no escape. There is no euphemism for my new purchase, no "eye patch" or "sun shield"; this decadent item is made to protect the eyes from things much more dangerous and tempting than the sun. It has nestled in its tissue paper lair for the last three months, carried everywhere I go, waiting for the perfect opportunity to be unleashed, not on an unsuspecting victim, but only on the most willing of participants. And there she is, Anastasia, the girl who has finally come along to fit that particular bill.

She whirls around the dance floor, into and out of the arms of many a lucky guy. She occasionally flashes me a blinding smile, all white teeth, blazing green eyes flashing, while I sit with my drink, my purse in my lap, waiting. We're both content with this division of labour as she dances her heart out and I get to watch her in action.

When I first saw the blindfold, I held it, fondled it really, revelling in its softness. I knew if I had a cock, I'd have wanted to fuck it; wanted to wrap my hard meat within its tender folds; to caress myself with its sensuous surface, probably lose control and cover it with my come before I ever knew what was happening — *that's* how gorgeous this blindfold is. Now I press it against the dick that feels just as real as any guy's that's nestled beneath my skirt, slim yet sturdy. I am stroking myself as casually as I can. And because I'm a girl with my own long curls, glowing lips, and stacked heels, I get away with this forbidden foreplay, and with planning what I will do with all that is in my lap once I get her home. And no one around me is the wiser. I'm simply a girl having a drink and waiting for her friend, rather than a creature planning the intricate tortures I'll make her submit to once we are alone.

Finally, hours later, she is ready to go. Her eyes have been smoldering at me from across the room, blazing a path through the throng of dancers as she lifts her dress just so, from lower to upper thigh, in a way that's clearly an invitation. I simply cross my legs in my lap and smile back. She'll have to come to get me, and eventually she does. I don't mind the time that has passed, for it has given me innumerable opportunities to observe her at play, to watch her curls flare out around her head, to get glimpses of her legs as her flouncy dress rose higher up her thigh, to imagine what she will look like splayed out across my bed. The hours of dancing and sitting respectively have worked us both into a frenzy, so once the door closes, it's anything goes.

We fall on each other like lovers separated for a lifetime, rather than girls who've been skirting our passion for a few weeks with coy glances and suggestive innuendo, neither bold enough to make that fateful first move. I press her face-first against the wall and slide my leg along the crack of her ass as she presses back against me. In a flash, I unzip her dress and bite the soft, tender flesh of her neck. I drag her over to the bed and push her down onto it before climbing on top of her. Nothing has prepared me for the beauty before me as we lay together in a lusty, sweaty heap, her face bathed in the glow of the tired but not yet sated. It is all there in her eyes, those eyes that beg for me to take her, to complete what I've started, to make us one. I press a hand between her legs, press the sheer, delicate cloth of her dress against her dripping cunt, hold it there as I marvel at how damp she is, how ripe and ready. I ease one finger inside her panties, along her slit, slow as can be, a tickle, a twirl, a tease. She bites her lower lip, holding back the words she wants to call out but doesn't. By unspoken agreement, she is silent, telling me what she wants with her searching stare and open legs. I am torn between those sparkling green globes and my precious plan. When my finger enters her just slightly but enough to make her moan, her eyes shut tight, I know that it's time. I pull her into a sitting position, grab a handful of bouncing, boisterous curls, and ease her head back, her eyes still closed, offering herself to me. I lean closer, lick the delicate skin of her neck that she bares, push my knee in between her legs and keep it there, both a warning and a promise.

Without me telling her, she knows that I want her to stay still, to let me decide what will happen next. I take another brief taste of her neck as she struggles not to squirm against me. I trace my fingers over her face, the smooth brow, the delicate eyelids, flushed cheeks, and bright pink lips. Then I reach for the blindfold, careful not to shake as I place it on her for the first time. She assents, and it looks just as beautiful there as I'd imagined. I ease off her dress and then her bra and panties and suddenly she's splayed out before me as a lovely specimen of womanhood.

"You're going to stay still for me, right?" I ask. "You look gorgeous right now. I like seeing your pussy. I've been thinking about it all night." She shudders in response and I move closer, whisper directly into her ear, "You like not being able to see, don't you? Because I could do anything I want to you, anything at all and you won't know until it's happening. And believe me, there's plenty that I'm going to do you; I had a long time to think about it while you were dancing. Spread your legs really wide for me." And she does, giving me a perfect view of her delicately shaved pussy, bearing only the lightest of fuzz. "Good girl," I say. "I like that you take directions well." I trace my fingers along her slit again, then leave them there. "What do you think I should do with your pussy, Anastasia? What should I fill you up with? Hmmm?" She can only moan in response and I pinch her clit between my fingers, hard enough so she'll still feel it once I let go. Then I turn her over onto her stomach and push her legs apart, stretching them wide so I have a perfect view of her ass and cunt.

I have to restrain myself from attacking her ferociously. I want to take this slowly if I can, as much for her sake as my own. I slide a finger along her juicy slit and am rewarded with another moan. I leave my finger pressed there while I survey her again. Without my even asking, her hands automatically move into position together behind her back. I clamp my hand around her wrists and push them against her back. I can't stand the sight of her perfectly curved, tanned ass in front of me and must slap it. Her breath comes out in a gasp of wondrous recognition, so I know she's been spanked before. But this time will be different. I slap her cheeks again, harder, my hand feeling the sting after each smack, then stop abruptly and thrust my thumb into her pussy while the rest of my hand splays itself across her ass, a finger teasing the delicate hole there that seems to be waiting for me. She wiggles beneath me, lets out a tortured sigh as I move only slightly. "Is there something you want, princess? I'm not going fast enough for you? You just can't wait for me to fuck you, isn't that right? I know what you want, but because you're acting so impatient, you're going to have to wait until I'm ready. And who knows when that will be. Do you want my cock, is that what you're telling me?" I ask, a hint of venom in my voice as I press her wrists against her back with a little more force.

"Yes, yes, that's what I want, please," she says, the words coming fast, tumbling out of her mouth in her need to appease me. I reach for the rope under the bed and tie her wrists together, in such a hurry that I forego the formality of pretty knots for a simply sturdy one, watch as she presses against them, her straining making both of us wetter. I press against my cock and feel a shiver of excitement spread throughout my body. I undress and hold out the cock to her lips, and they part seamlessly, sucking it in as I push against her, and that sight of her — covered in the purple velvet, lips open in pure desire, hands bound, and body tensed — is enough and I come in a sharp, silent shudder. I pull out and she looks up at me, and I know if I could see her eyes they'd express an echo of disappointment at the loss of my cock to suck.

Not for long, though. I grab her hair at the nape of her neck and pull sharp and tight. "You like sucking cock, don't you?" I ask. "You like letting me use your mouth like that, don't you?" As I ask her these rhetorical questions, I stroke her slit again and am amazed at how wet she is. I had suspected, knew even, that it turned her on, but as my fingers practically glide into her of their own accord, I know she's more than ready. I pull out, roll a condom onto my fat cock, and settle myself between her legs, as excited as any teenage boy to finally sink inside her wet, willing heat. I hold my cock for a minute, press the tip of it against her cunt, and watch her squirm. "Stay still," I bark, even though I like the way her ass looks when she moves, but I feel a heady rush when she immediately stills, her hands clutching the sheets as if to keep herself steady. I push into her and feel her tighten around me instantly. I can't resist and push all the way inside and lean forward so I'm pressed up against her back and bite into her neck again as I fuck her slow but hard. Then I sit up, the better to look at her gyrating body about to fall apart beneath me. I push her legs apart by the ankles, watch as the shudders pass through her body, as she strains to move against the rope, against me, against her own will to remain still and let me control the pace. But she can't help it, it's like the music is still in her blood, only now I get to see her do a very different kind of dance, one that ends as she comes in a fierce, wracking orgasm that makes her cry out, her fingers flexing to try to grab me, to grab anything she can. I pull out and hold her hand, squeeze it tight while with my other hand I reach under the cock and, with a few quick strokes, bring myself to an orgasm that has me crashing down against her, spent. I kiss her back, my own private dancing queen, rocking to a beat that's all our own.

A QUIET EVENING AT HOME

Trish Kelly

The dishes are done, the laundry basket is empty, and I'm sitting at the table while you divide the sushi onto two plates. Thursday is your night to take care of dinner, so the counter is covered with takeout from the Japanese place down the block.

I'm wearing a miniskirt with no underwear, but you haven't notice yet. Actually, you seem kind of distracted this evening, which annoys me more than it should. I'm on a new hormone pill for my "bacne," and my pussy has been swollen all day. I've fucked myself with the egg vibrator you gave me and two shampoo bottles during my extra long "shower" today.

You place a bowl of salty green soybeans on the table and I realize I'm hungry.

You return to the kitchen for a tube of wasabi, and I unbutton my shirt a little more.

Many of the bois I've known have fought hard against their bodies, binding their breasts, layering their shirts, but you don't have to do that; it's as if your body caught the signals in time and decided not to burden you with breasts. Sometimes I catch you talking to my chest, and I place my finger under your chin and tilt your head back up to my face. I always click my tongue with mock disapproval, which makes you sheepish. But I won't do that tonight.

My pussy has started a new habit of drooling, which I blame on the extra hormones in my body. I worry that I'll seep right through my miniskirt before you even sit down.

But here you are, back at the table with a plate of my favourite *maki*.

You take your first soybean and crack it in your mouth. The coarse salt sticks to your fingers as you take the next.

"How's your fish?" you ask.

"Fresh," I say.

You finish another bean and reach for your napkin, but I stop you. I lean across the table, using my elbows to push my breasts together, and take your hand and lick the salt from your palm. Then I take your first two fingers in my mouth and suck the salt off them too.

Your eyes grow large for a moment, perhaps surprised by the level of suction, the eagerness of my tongue, and so I release you.

"Whoa," you say, your voice cracking. The cracking is new. I think it's cute, but you're obviously embarrassed by it.

Your decision to go on T was a big one. There were many things lost because of the decision, the right to play on the women's hockey team and the reaction from your family among them. But when we talked about it, you conceded that you needed to feel like you were in control.

But you can't control the voice cracking even though you knew it might happen, and no one can say if it will go away or if your voice will always be stuck in this transition from boy to man.

I ignore the crack in your voice and pick up my chopsticks. "How was work?" I inquire.

"Good," you reply, your eyes on my chest, and I know I've got you. You've just had your T shot, which makes it an easy win for me. The shots make you horny, or violent, sometimes both.

You toss a few more soybean shells in the bowl and then put your fingers in my mouth again. Your other hand goes to the nape of my neck.

You wrap your fingers in my hair and pull me toward you until I'm kneeling on my chair, my ass stuck in the air for balance and my breasts resting on the plate in front of you. I run my tongue along the bottom of your fingers, cleaning off all the salt in the cracks of your work-worn calluses. I try to make eye contact, but your gaze is fixed on my tits. I bob my head on your fingers, bouncing on my chair so my tits hit the table. I know it's a good show because your fingers tighten in my hair. I suck hard on your fingers like I'm blowing your biggest cock. Since you started hormone therapy, my blowjobs have improved vastly.

"I wanna see those lips wrapped around something besides my finger," you say, pushing your plate to the other end of the table. I feign surprise, like this is your idea.

You pull me across the table so that I'm actually lying on my plate, and the smell of seaweed fills my nose as you get up and walk behind me. I feel my skirt rising like a curtain at a dirty picture show and then hear your deep groan of pleasure when my skirt sits on my hips. I feel your fingers tracing my wetness from my thighs to the edge of my pussy.

"I invite you for a nice dinner and you drip all over my dining room chair?" you say. Your voice climbs without breaking, the bravado grounding it so that you sound like any biological man about to beat his woman's ass.

Then I feel the first slap. I have a high pain tolerance, which is lucky for me. The gym has become a favourite place for you lately, a place where you easily pass, a place where you watch yourself bulk up and no one questions you. I can't see your arms, but I know they are bulging with effort as you hit my ass again.

"I'm deeply sorry," I say, and raise my ass in the air.

"Slut." I hear, and then you hit me again with such force, I think I can feel the pattern of your fingerprints embedding in my flesh.

I sneak a look over my shoulder, and your left hand is in your pants.

Through your open fly, I can see flashes of your fuchsia pink cock, the one with the raised bumps on the tip.

"What are you looking at?" you snarl, and I turn away.

My pussy is dripping down to my knees now. Your strikes are getting very close to the lips of my cunt. This is where you always stop, at the threshold of beating my pussy. You give me two more hard slaps, and then I hear your belt come out of the loops of your pants.

My breath catches at the thought of more beats. I whimper, and then I hear you kick off your pants. You nudge my shoulder, and I stand up dizzily. Your cock bobs in front of me, adding to my sense of motion. You sit down at the head of the table, and I feel like I'm falling as I lower myself to the floor. I kneel in front of your cock, and rest my arms in your lap as I try to gain my balance.

"Don't be a cocktease," you warn, grabbing me by the arm. I take your cock in my mouth, making sure to cheat the angle so that you can see the action. I'm sucking it in as far as I can, trying to make my forehead touch your six pack. I make it on the third attempt, and you let out a big sigh. The deeper you breathe, the easier it is for me to make contact with your belly.

Your lap smells sharply of latex and pussy juice, but I can't say anything about it because my mouth is full of cock. You're rocking your hips so hard that most girls would be gagging by now. The veins in your forearms are sticking out and you're trying to grab my tits, so I slide your dick out of my mouth and climb into your lap.

I'm so slippery you have to hold onto me. I reach behind me with one hand and dig under the harness to find your pussy.

It's hard for you to concentrate, so I'm doing most of the work now. My fingers are plunging in you as I slide up and down on your pole. "My man likes it when I play with his balls, doesn't he?" I ask.

You begin to contract around my fingers, and your nails dig into my ass as you start the climb. I'm whimpering in pain and pleasure and it makes you thrash under me. You bite my neck and it sends me over. My back arches and there is a moment of complete stillness for both of us. Then you look at me and start to laugh. I look down at my shirt. It is covered in wasabi and sticky rice.

"We'd better clean you up," you say, and sit me on the table before leaving to run me a bath. My ass stings, but I think I can take a bit more. I get up and follow you to the bathroom.

PRISM

Anna Camilleri

My first week in Vancouver, I discovered one of the local dyke hangouts: a bookstore and coffee bar on Commercial Drive nestled amongst grocery stores, billiard halls, and restaurants. I was having a smoke out front when someone in a rust-patched pick-up pulled up. She jumped out, smiled my way, and sauntered in as though she owned the joint. Her straw-coloured hair shot straight out in cross-hatched diagonals; the collar of her denim jacket was turned inside, work boot tongues stuck out from the bottom of her cords, and rumpled scraps of papers flapped out of her back pocket. I breathed in her woody scent as she blew past — she smelled like the kind of trouble I like, and that I had sworn off of a dozen times — hints of top-soil and pot, layered with aftershave. Coastal air, heavy with wet and tree bark and salt residue, carries a scent trail a long, long way.

I went back inside where she turned to me and offered a firm hand. "My name's Jo." Then she told me she was a landscaper and that she would run away with the circus someday. I told her I had just managed to get my legs feeling right again after a five-day drive across Canada, and that I'd never seen mountains before driving through Alberta.

"Oh, yeah?" She rolled a toothpick between her front teeth, like she was in no hurry.

"Where'd ya come from, besides out of the blue?"

"Toronto."

"Oh, yeah. Big city girl, eh?" I sensed she had a lot more to say on the subject, and I was sure I would hear at least some of it before long.

"Yeah, it's a big city." The wooden stir stick I'd been nervously twirling flew out of my hand and landed in Jo's hair. "Oh God, I'm sorry!" I said.

"Let me get —"

She tilted her head forward and the stir stick landed in my lap. "Thought you might want that back."

"Thanks." I set it down on the counter next to my empty mug. Thanks? I felt like an idiot. I was going to ask Jo if Vancouver was her home, but the moment was gone, which was just as well. I could hear her say something like "Don't I look at home?" and I'd respond with a brilliant one-liner like, "Yeah, sure." Then I'd bumble along with, "I didn't mean anything … I was just making conversation."

Jo pulled the toothpick out of her mouth swiftly as if she just remembered she had somewhere else to be. "You like stories?"

"Yeah, I love a good story." I settled on the creaky stool, telling myself not to fall off.

"A good story? Okay, I'll dial up a *good* story." Jo disappeared into the dusty book stacks. I had just finished counting the coffee grounds in the bottom of my mug when she sat next to me again, but closer this time.

"Ready?" she asked. I noticed a delicate pouch of skin that gathered in the centre of her upper lip, like a widow's peak, only on her mouth. I nodded.

Not fifteen minutes had passed since we had set eyes on each other, and I was positive the circus would find Jo; she wouldn't need to go looking. She gave me a quick wink and produced a Dr Seuss book from behind her back. She leaned in until her left shoulder and my right shoulder touched, and I watched her mouth while she sounded words with a hint of an Irish lilt. She kept focused on the page, looking up just long enough to catch my eye and shift in her seat. With each shift in weight or footing on our stools, we returned to contact; shoulder touching shoulder, kneecap touching kneecap. I noticed a trace of magnolia on her, of a young tree just before the heavy blooms fall away.

Even before she whispered *Sam I Am* — before she uttered a word — I was sunk. Was it her rumpled collar, the way she rolled the toothpick between her teeth, coughed and read all at the same time, or the sweetness of being read a story in the middle of the afternoon, in the middle of a coffee bar with people milling around? I was love-struck.

Jo closed the book with a snap. "Nice little story, eh?'

"Yeah, really nice." I drew the mug to my mouth, and not one bitter

drop wetted my tongue. "I keep thinking there's more coffee in the cup …
I finished it a while ago."

"You wanna 'nother?"

"No, thanks. I think I'd vibrate right off the stool."

Jo smirked. "I'd like to see that." We both laughed out loud.

"Wanna blow this joint?"

"Sure." We left with at least six pairs of eyes on our backs. I sensed Jo
was the dyke equivalent of the welcome-wagon.

Jo climbed into the pick-up. There was a pile of chocolate bar wrappers
and empty coffee cups on the passenger seat.

"I'll just move that out of the way." Jo stuffed the wrappers and cups
in the gap between the seat and the window and wiped crumbs from the
seat with her shirt sleeve. "There's a seat for you, my lady."

"Thanks." I climbed in.

"So, where do you wanna go?" That same smirk danced on Jo's face.

"I like surprises."

We lit smokes, and Jo popped in a tape. It was Simon and Garfunkel,
which surprised me, but I couldn't say why.

Jo looked over at me. "I like a good tune."

I nodded. "When were you born?"

"'69 — year of the Rooster."

"What do you mean?"

"Year of the Rooster, you know — Chinese astrology."

"Oh." I didn't know anything about Chinese astrology.

"Roosters are supposed to be funny and hot-headed," she said.

I smiled. "Sounds like trouble. Are you?"

"Depends on what you mean by trouble." She winked at me.

"Okay … well, you're funny."

"Yeah, I like to think so."

"And humble too." We laughed in unison.

Jo turned up the volume and sang along, one eyebrow cocked: "Cecelia,
you're breaking my heart. You're shaking my confidence daily. Oh Cecelia,
I'm down on my knees, I'm begging you please to come home. Come on
home."

I sang back, "Making love in the afternoon with Cecelia up in my bedroom. I got up to wash my face. When I come back to bed, someone's taken

my place." We harmonized while we drove over a bridge, and then another. Before long, the trees were taller and greener. We drove around sharp bends; a wall of amber rock was on my right, and on my left, the biggest houses I'd ever seen. And then, an explosion of deep blue. We parked.

"Is that the Pacific?" I asked.

"Sure is — pretty, eh?"

"Beautiful." I reached for her mouth, gently stroked the pouch of skin on her upper lip. "I like your lips."

Jo's cheeks coloured and she leaned in closer. "Can I kiss you?"

I replied without a word. Her mouth was as soft as it looked and her tongue, velvet. She traced the skin under my chin to my collarbone. My breath caught.

"Is this okay?"

"Mmm-hmm. You feel good."

"Do you want some dinner?"

The question jarred me. "Umm, sure."

"I don't have much at my place — I can make us some tea and toast."

"Your place?"

Her face lit up with wickedness. "Yeah, my place." She winked at me. "Want some toast?"

"I'd love some toast."

At Jo's apartment, she inserted the key in the door and turned back toward me. "Just to warn ya, my place is a mess."

I nodded.

We walked around her kitchen table, stacked with newspapers and take-out food containers, and then down the hallway into the livingroom/bedroom. Jo cleared a place for me to sit on the couch. "Thanks," I said, but instead of sitting, I walked across the room to a cluster of black-and-white photographs. I pointed to a picture of a child who was standing on a dock, holding up a big fish. "Is that you?"

"Yeah, my gramps says that was my first catch," Jo said.

"You look pretty happy with yourself."

Jo walked over to the photograph. "Yeah, I guess I was."

"And are you happy with yourself right now?" I tugged at Jo's collar.

She flushed with colour again. "Yeah, I feel pretty good."

I pulled her toward me and ran my tongue along the blonde down above her upper lip.

"You taste like you smell," I said.

Jo tapped the radiator nervously. "Bad?"

I shook my head. "Good," I said. I ran my tongue along the inside of her lower lip, and placed my hand on the back of her head. I kissed her deep and listened to the rhythm of her breath as it slowed and caught. I tugged at Jo's belt buckle.

She pulled back slightly. "I thought you were shy."

"Do you want me to be shy?" I teased.

Jo beamed. "No — I mean, I just thought you were."

"Right now I'm not." I pulled my top and my bra up over my head. "Would you like some help out of your clothes?" I asked.

"No, I'm good right now." Jo stepped toward me. "But I like you naked." She cupped my breasts and stroked my nipples with her thumbs. I pressed my knee into her crotch and her breath came faster.

I whispered into her ear. "I want you to fuck me." Jo took me by the hand and led me to her bed. She pushed the hair out of my face and tongued my nipple. I moaned. She slid open the bedside table and pulled out a harness and dildo.

I reached for her. "That's not what I want — I want your hand inside me."

Jo looked pleased and pulled on a latex glove. She reached for the lube as I wriggled out of my pants. She knelt between my legs and stroked my cunt. I arched my back and spread my legs wider. She applied more pressure at the base of my cunt. I clasped her hair as she entered me with two fingers. I pushed against her. "I want you inside me. I'll open for you."

She squeezed lube into her palm and slid more of her hand into me. My cunt took her in down to the wide part of her hand. I imagined myself opening like a Venus flytrap. I relaxed my muscles and took in her whole fist. A prism of heat and colour burst open.

"Yes." I bucked against her.

"Do you like this?" she teased and fucked me faster.

I closed my eyes and wrapped my legs around her. I gave myself over to my body, her hand, our heat. I rushed toward an exit, my body careening through a passage that amplified sound as if to point to a speck of light in the distance. I slowed my breath and stroked my own breasts. I imagined the tunnel widening. I pulled her tighter and pressed my cunt down onto her hand as I gasped for air.

"Do you want me out?" she asked as she stroked my face.

I touched her arm and shook my head. She pumped in and out of me with a slower, more measured rhythm. I bore down on her. We stayed like this until my cunt clamped tight around her hand as I came. We looked at each other, suspended, until I reached down and motioned for her to pull out.

She collapsed next to me, lit a smoke, and pressed it to my lips. I took a long haul and rolled into her. Jo was still fully clothed.

I tugged at her shirt tail. "You still want these clothes on?" I asked.

Jo smiled and said, "I'm warming up."

We stayed in her apartment for two days before we came up for air. Sleep, food, and water deprivation — combined with a steady diet of cigarettes, coffee, dry toast, and sex — caused a delirium that made us fast girlfriends, which is the wrong word, but it'll have to do.

We carried on for three months. At the end of it all, we nodded uncomfortably at one another from across rooms and streets for a year before we spoke again. We became friends, eventually.

Thirteen years have now passed since the day Jo pulled up in a pickup. She did join the circus, and later, ran away from it, and I've driven across the Rockies a dozen times since then — twice with Jo.

That afternoon with Jo reminds me that touch is good, and that sometimes, love doesn't know its own name, but lust is sure-footed and can come swiftly and surprisingly, when you least expect it.

FORTUNATE MESSES

Amber Dawn

Pamela, Kay, and Tia-Lee sit together on the fake leather chaise in the lobby. The front door, propped open by one of Pamela's stiletto boots, lets in the cool night and the curtains billow in the breeze like black lace ghosts. It is quiet, so quiet they can hear the mechanical billboard outside squeak as it changes from the new McCombo meal ad, to the lottery ad, to the breast cancer awareness ad, and then back to the new McCombo again.

"This night's a bust," Pamela says, taking the almost empty bottle of Crown from Kay's hand. The bottle, a gift from one of Kay's clients that night, had been shared among the three of them for the last hour. Pamela, her wispy red hair sticking to her lips as she swallows, unflinchingly finishes it off. "Why don't you come outside with us, Kay? It's been good money."

"I already broke three times tonight. I'm good."

"What are you saying? You were in the back reading the whole night."

"She had three," says Tia-Lee. "She could have had four. She turned one away."

"What's wrong with you, girl?" asks Pamela, her hands fly up in the air. "I keep hearing 'bout you turning down money. You trying to square up, or what?"

"I got to finish this chapter for school tomorrow."

"Right," Pamela says, rolling her eyes. "How long you been in school now?"

"Three years."

"So why now all of a sudden we hardly see you?"

"I haven't worked outside for a year, Pam. Why do you bother asking anymore? I'm busy enough in here."

"Your new man won't let you, will he?"

"I'm just not feelin' it anymore, you know what I'm sayin'?" Kay's chest tightens like it always does when girls from work ask anything about her personal life. In particular, her boyfriend Owen is not a topic open for discussion.

"You didn't answer me," says Pamela, leaning towards Kay. "I said, does your man let you outside or not?"

"What's it to you?" Tia-Lee pipes in. "She don't ask you 'bout your jacked-up man. I see him downtown, making the rounds in his wanna-be Armani suit. That's why she's on you, Kay. She wants to bring you home to Daddy so he can turn you out for himself."

"Shhh, don't be tellin' the dumb bitch my plan," Pamela laughs, and the three of them kick at each other with their bare feet and pretend to pull each other's hair, shouting "cocksucker," "nastybitch," "skidmark," "cumbreath," and "whore," until Kay falls backwards off the chaise. The floor is cold and sticky, but she is too dizzy to get up. She watches Tia-Lee and Pamela sloppily fix their hair-pieces and lipstick. Tia-Lee's g-string peeks out from her white low-cut jeans. For a moment Kay loses herself in the rhinestone heart appliquéd on the back of Tia-Lee's panties. Her pelvic muscles tighten involuntarily and she looks away. Kay can count on one hand the number of times she has been turned on at work. She makes a point of not allowing herself sexual feelings, so much so that it has carried over into her everyday life. She's gone weeks without masturbating, never mind sex. She decides the recent tickle between her legs is entirely Owen's doing. He has awoken something in her. Kissing him alone makes her hotter than the sex she's had with the last half dozen men, or women for that matter. And Owen hasn't even fucked her yet.

For over two months now it's been all dinners, movies, and discussions about the dinners and movies. It has been campus lectures, jogs along the seawall, and fully clothed make-out sessions on Kay's living room sofa. The illusion of romantic innocence wavered only momentarily the night Kay told Owen how she makes her money. They were at a late-night screening of *Last Exit to Brooklyn* at the Ridge Theatre and something about seeing Jennifer Jason Leigh hustle sailors made Kay blurt it out as the credits were rolling. She waited for Owen to walk out or get angry or both. The house lights went up, and in the empty theatre he kissed her forehead. "I already knew what you do for work," he said calmly. "A guy from my rowing team told me. And I saw your photo on the Lolita's website." They stared at each other for what seemed like a lifetime. A hundred questions paraded through Kay's mind, and her jaw began to tremble.

Owen held her face in his hands. "If you are wondering if that is why I haven't tried to sleep with you yet, it's not," he said. "It's because I was born female. I'm transsexual. I didn't know how you would handle it."

The Ken and Barbie facade was only fortified by this disclosure. Instead of asking questions or starting discussions, Kay simply started wearing pink more often, as if embellishing the softer side of her own gender might somehow comfort him. For him, Kay now puts on a good girl smile, curbs her swearing, and uses "I" statements instead of threatening violence when she's angry.

Owen responded by opening doors, running her baths, and holding her tiny hand in the crook of his elbow like he was never going to let go. Together they laughed harder, jogged further, and had more insightful discussions, even food tasted better, or at least they put more effort into the tasting.

In private, Kay read and re-read the few FTM support websites she could find on the Internet. She discovered Owen doing his own reading when she found a dog-eared copy of *Whores and Other Feminists* tucked under his pillow. They never talked about it. Or when they tried to talk about it, they would somehow end up discussing Foucault or the Marquis de Sade instead.

All this avoidance makes Kay pent up with wanting. At this moment, she wonders if Pamela and Tia-Lee would notice if she put her hand down her pants and touched herself right there on the lobby floor. Just as the thought crosses her mind, her phone vibrates inside her pocket. "I'm out of here," she says as she pulls herself up and stumbles across the room. Pamela rushes towards her as she heads for the door.

"He's good to you, right, girl?" Pamela asks. "I mean, as good as a man can be." She peers out the door at the old Volkswagen pulled up out front, her arms folded in front of her.

"Yeah, he is good," Kay tells her, giving Pam's shoulder a little squeeze before walking away. She hopes Owen doesn't see Pamela hanging out of the doorway in her red, see-through work clothes. She hopes her mouth tastes more like wintermint gum than whiskey and that her skin smells nothing like the latex/scented-candle/man stench of the massage parlour.

Once inside Owen's car, Kay smiles in the vanity mirror and pulls her hair back into a clumsy ponytail with a faux-fur scrunchy. "How was work?" Owen asks. Tonight, this normal question hits her like a kick to the head.

"Why do you come here?" she asks in return. "I never asked you to be pickin' me up." Just like that her "good-girl" spell is broken. A tear slips from the corner of her eye. All of her doubt, confusion, fears, and unspoken questions rush in; she can feel her skull welling up with pressure. She tries to stop the flood of alcohol and stress-induced self-deprecations from spilling out of her mouth, but it's too late. The monologue of hate has already begun. Somewhere between "You're too good for me" and "Where exactly is this relationship going," Kay realizes Owen has driven down an alleyway and turned off the ignition.

"Do you want to come sit on my lap?" he asks, shifting his seat back. For a moment, she resists this offer, but in truth, his welcoming lap is the only place she wants to be right now. She barely nods yes, and Owen starts to remove her tight terrycloth track pants as she comes to him. He places one hand gently on her neck and the other inside her panties, and feels her throat tremble as she quietly cries and her pussy opens, so slightly, with wetness.

"You know that I want you," he tells her. Kay hears the way he emphasizes "you" and looks up at him.

"Why?" She knows her voice is still trembling and that her question may even sound childish. But something inside her, childlike or not, needs to know why.

"I can't remember the last time someone has been on my mind so much," he says. "That's why I come get you after work, because I want you to be the last person I see; the last thought I have before going to sleep. I can't really explain it."

He traces little circles above her clit: this is all the explanation she needs. She grabs hold of his shirt and exhales deeply into the soft cotton fabric. One of his buttons comes undone and her fingertips find, for the first time, his warm skin. Sliding her hand along his stomach, she undoes two more. She looks at him again, searches his face for any uneasiness, but there is only desire. The corners of Owen's mouth curl into a grin as she fumbles with the rest of his buttons. She opens his shirt and rests her head against him. His heart pounds inside his chest as if it wants to break out of his body. She presses her mouth to his skin. Her tongue follows a trail of fine hair up to his neck where she sinks her teeth for a moment. A cross between a yelp and a moan escapes Owen's lips. Kay drags her teeth and tongue along his collarbone, Owen's sounds encouraging her. She sucks and nibbles his shoulder, his flesh welting up in her mouth.

If she could, she'd swallow whole mouthfuls of him. She would choke on him and still keep sucking. She moves to his nipple, biting gently, then hard. Owen presses his lips together tight as she runs her fingernails across him, scratching along his scars as though she's felt them dozens of times before. He takes the pain for as long as he can, feeling her breath on him as she moans, his skin growing hot in her mouth, the prolonged sting after her teeth release him, and the burn of her nails. When he can take it no longer, he scoops up her legs and hoists them over his shoulders. She loses her balance for a second, then leans back against the steering wheel; the horn beeps a few times as she shifts into a comfortable position. He looks down at her pussy, parted and dripping, in his lap. Four of his fingers now work easily inside of her, his middle fingertip just touching her cervix. "You like that," she says. "You like fucking your girl." Owen sinks his hand a little deeper, his thumb firmly pressed to her clit. Kay's feet kick at the car ceiling. Her hands grab the dash behind her as she begins to scream. A small pool of cum spills into Owen's hand, then more. Even though it's been awhile, she knows this kind of orgasm: the water works, the super soaker. "Fuck," Kay says, reaching blindly around the passenger seat trying to find something to catch her ejaculate. She jerks herself up, but Owen holds her there as her cum rushes, seeping into his pants. "I'm sorry," she starts to say, feeling his wet jeans beneath her.

"I like a mess," he interrupts her. He puts his hand to his mouth and tastes her on his fingers. They kiss, passing her cum between their lips.

"You found my scars," says Owen.

"I think I felt something," she nods.

He reaches up and turns on the car light. "Here," he points to a thin set of scars an inch or two below his nipples. Kay squints her eyes as if looking off into the distance, then smiles at the adornment of teeth and nail marks on his skin. "I can't really see them in this light," she says. "All I can see is the marks I've left on you."

This is the beginning of something Kay and Owen consider extraordinary. Owen stops showing up at her door with cut flowers and instead dons an eight-inch strap-on. Their cinema of choice becomes a three-by-three-foot porn stall in the back of the all-night sex store. They eat Chinese delivery for three straight days, not once leaving Kay's apartment.

Owen discovers a deeply buried fetish for wearing women's lingerie. Kay develops a taste for ass fucking (especially in combination with the lingerie). Something about seeing him squeezed uncomfortably into her fishnet stockings makes her want to rip into them, spread his ass cheeks, and start rimming. She's come to love watching him squirm, just a bit, as she wraps her acrylic fingernails in soft clumps of tissue before putting on the glove, the thrill of his sphincter muscles completely relaxing around her fingers, and the smell of their hot and sloppy sex. Everything is like an offering to her, even scrubbing the cum spots soaked through the sheets onto the bare mattress makes her feel desire.

And like the jism soaking into the sheets, their afterglow bleeds into the rest of their lives. Things become easier. Kay notices it first at work. Lately, she barely has to flash her tits and clients are tipping extra; she can't even remember the last time a man called her a whore.

Then Owen's rowing team begins winning races, how effortlessly now his oars catch the water. After races, he and his teammates walk with their arms around each other's aching shoulders. All eight of them are getting along after months of petty and poorly communicated tensions. "You're my good luck charm," he tells Kay after a race.

She doesn't give it much thought until she gets an A on her "Villains and Virgins in Romantic Theatre" paper. She has never gotten an A in school, not even in fifth-grade arts and crafts class. As she glances at the enthusiastic scattering of red check-marks across the pages of her paper, she remembers poring over reference books naked while Owen lay under the table jerking off, asking her to spread her legs wider as she read.

When the phone call from his surgeon's office comes moments after fucking, Owen is convinced that they are somehow blessed. As he watches her yanking her jeans back on, he receives word that a cancellation has moved him up on the waiting list; his phallo appointment is now just four months away. "Hey ladybug, you really are bringing me good luck," he says, hanging up the phone. Kay claps her hands like an excited child at the news. If this luck lasts, she will be there through the whole healing process, maybe even wearing a slutty nurse costume and feeding him in bed. She will be the first one to hold his new cock in her thankful little hand. But more exciting than the thought of his virgin cock is the thought of just touching and tasting him. Kay has always respected Owen's choice to leave his genitalia out of their sexual arena — though that doesn't mean she hasn't privately fantasized about sucking him off.

The evening after Owen's surgeon calls, he drops her off at work, as usual, except this time he sits out front for a while, as if hypnotized by the blinking neon lights in the window. In his hand he keeps flipping open then closing his cell phone. Finally, he breaks down and calls her. "We should be celebrating," he says.

"I would walk outta here if I could," she tells him, her voice hushed. "Tomorrow we'll do the town up right, okay?"

Owen listens to the dial tone then lays his phone on the dash. He stares at it, hoping she'll call back, but it doesn't ring. He stares at the front door of Lolita's until it opens, but it isn't Kay. A man darts out instead. Owen watches him walk down the street. "You're being a creep," Owen tells himself and turns the key in the ignition. As he's about to pull away, he sees something drop out of the man's jacket pocket. It's money. He can't actually see from this distance, but his gut tells him it is money. The moral dilemma passes swiftly. Owen gets out of the car to retrieve the billfold. He counts it: $480. Who carries around that kind of money? Owen stands on the curb for a minute, then without giving it much thought, he turns and walks into Kay's workplace.

The walls are the colour of tomato soup. All of the furniture is black. A girl in a tube top and sarong comes over. "First time here?" she asks. Owen nods. He looks back towards the door and considers running out again. "You don't have to be nervous," she tells him. "I'm Candy. I'll help you get started. Massage prices begin at fifty dollars for a half-hour. Eighty for an hour. Tipping for extras is between you and your hostess. You understand?" Owen nods again. He tries to think of something to say, but before he can a group of six women in swimwear enter the room and arrange themselves, smiling, in front of him.

Kay is there, looking stunned yet gorgeous in a black bikini and long black opera gloves. He stares at her, still reaching for something to say. She looks back at him only long enough for him to see she's angry, then she fixes her gaze firmly at the front entrance. "You like this one?" Candy asks, draping her arm around Kay. "She's really friendly. I'll just collect your room fee, then you can meet your hostess in one of our fantasy rooms." All of the women parade away except Candy, who wordlessly pulls eighty dollars from the billfold in Owen's trembling hand and firmly ushers him into a room and shuts the door. He is alone in a dark bedroom, lit only with candles and a big screen TV playing porn. Kay enters the room, mutes the sound on the video, and asks, "What exactly do you think you are doing?"

"I'm not sure," he says honestly. "This guy dropped some money as he was leaving here. And so suddenly I had a nice amount of free money. I guess I could have tried to give it back to him."

"Whatever to that! I've only been here twenty minutes and already I've had to deal with two belligerent assholes. The last guy didn't make it past the lobby before we had to throw him out. Be glad you got that trick's money. How much did you find?" Owen spreads out three $100 bills and two fifties on the bedside table. Her eyes widen. "Why don't you just keep it? You can give your doctor another payment. If you go now I can probably get your eighty dollars back."

"I don't know, Kay," he says. "Isn't this a place where men come to feel good about themselves?"

"I should think that your *girlfriend* keeps you feeling good enough," Kay says sharply.

She sits down on the bed and blankly watches a penis slap against two fake breasts on the TV. Owen wrestles with words, wanting to say something to make this whole situation over. Before he can reply, Kay says, "I know you've shared a lot with me. I get that. But this —" She motions around the room with her hand. "— is private. You're not meant to see it. I really don't know why you came in here."

"I was sitting in the car, just sitting there thinking about how I wanted to be with you tonight so badly. And when that guy dropped his money it was like an answer from some greater force. As if something heard me wanting you and then, *poof*, gave me a way to be close to you."

"But why here, in this place?"

"It doesn't matter where we are."

Kay turns toward Owen. She locks eyes with him, studying his face.

"Okay, to be honest," Owen says, "maybe it does matter. All these guys need is a bit of cash and they can breeze in and out of fantasy land, or wherever, for that matter." Owen pauses for a second. Kay sees him struggling with words, and she softens a bit. "I'm being selfish," he says, defeated. "I'll go."

"Wait." Kay stands and wraps her arms around him. "I can't think of a man more deserving of a bit of good, old-fashioned carnal illusion. If that is what you want?" He shrugs his shoulders like a guilty child; the left corner of his mouth curls in a shy grin.

"Well, since it's free money anyway, why don't you make it worth your time," she says. "We could get another girl in here and give you what we call a duo full-body massage. Basically, we get naked and oily and rub ourselves all over you."

"Are you fuckin' serious?" Owen's thigh muscles twitch with sudden excitement, and he starts to pace the room. "I can barely drop my drawers in front of you."

"You don't have to. Lots of guys don't. I'll bring in this girl Sherri, she looks exactly like Nina Hardley from those *Adam and Eve* movies you like."

Owen opens his mouth to deny his lust for the blonde porn star, but his curiosity gets the better of him. "How much does she look like her?"

Kay motions Owen to sit beside her. "I can't believe we're doing this," she says. "One thing: never break from the game. You don't know me. I don't know you. And, you'll want to take off your shirt and pants." Then she gets up and leaves the room.

The wall behind the bed is one large mirror; Owen watches himself undress before a backdrop of porn. On the screen, he sees a close-up of a penis teasing pussy, slapping it, butting its head up against a clit, tracing awkward circles. Before the moment of penetration, Owen presses the power button off and the room darkens. His eyes readjust and he finds himself again in the mirror. Candlelight illuminates his wiry muscles; he flexes his arms. Hearing women's voices in the hallway, he quickly adjusts his black boxer shorts and poses himself on the bed. As promised Kay returns with another woman. "I'm Sherri," she says in a high-pitched voice. Her large lips are outlined with dark lip liner and her mouth does not close all the way even after she stops talking.

She and Kay crawl onto the bed and kneel on either side of him. Two pairs of long, slender fingers reach for each other over his body. Sherri unhooks the front clasp of Kay's bikini with one hand. In the other she shakes a bottle, flips open the lid, and squeezes. Massage oil flies in a high arc through the air, landing like a bull's eye in Kay's cleavage. Sherri starts to run her hands over Kay from shoulders to stomach, Kay's breasts bouncing from the friction. "Oh, I want to be topless too," says Sherri. Her voice, still cartoonish, has dropped an octave or so. Leaning forward, she rests her torso across him. Her hair tickles him as she nuzzles against his body like an animal marking its prey. Kay gives Owen a little wink as she unties Sherri's string bikini. Sherri sits up like a cat stretching, pressing her body into Kay's, and the two women rub themselves together like a bridge of writhing and glistening flesh over him. If Owen squints his eyes, he can barely make out where one body stops and another begins. Still tangled, they slowly descend upon him, writhing up and down his body. He imagines a tide of nipples, hair, lips, legs, and hipbones washing over him. Like a drowning man he reaches up, not knowing what he can grab onto. "It's okay," says Sherri, leaning over him on all fours. "You can touch us." Owen doesn't move. His actions haven't caught up with his mind. "Don't worry. Nothing is going to happen unless you want it to," she says, and places his hand on her left tit.

"This doesn't happen to you every day," Kay whispers in his ear. Owen takes a deep breath and sits up. He can feel a tiny but growing wet spot in his boxers. He considers leaving now; he could be dressed and jerking off in the car within five minutes.

"What else can I do for you?" Sherri asks, leaning over him. She traces his lips with her nipple.

"Be my inspiration," he says without hesitation. "I want you to go sit on that chair over there and masturbate while this beautiful girl right here gives me a blowjob." Owen turns to Kay, her jaw open and eyes wide.

"We'd be happy to do that for you," Kay manages to say. She kneels on the floor and motions for him to sit on the edge of the bed in front of her. Sherri drags out a tiny desktop lamp from behind a potted fake bamboo. She situates herself, long legs spread and back arched, on a tiny, leopard-print chair a few feet away, then points the lamp, like a mini-spotlight, between her legs. From her purse, she fishes out a gold vibrator and lifts it to her lips. Kay removes Owen's boxers, scratching his legs as she slides them down. She looks up at him, watches his eyes move from down at her to Sherri's toy show. Behind her, the vibrator begins buzzing.

Kay knows Sherri is watching them too. For everyone's benefit, she must act with Owen like she would with any other client. She reaches for a condom and tears open the wrapper. But instead of rolling it over Owen, as she would a client, she sneaks the condom onto her index and middle fingers and presses them lightly on Owen's asshole.

Kay feels certain that from Sherri's perspective everything looks like a "normal date," only now she's not about to suck a latex covered stranger or tickle unfamiliar balls to get her client to cum faster. Only Kay knows just how much she has hungered for this moment. She opens her mouth and takes him in. The taste of salt hits the back of her throat. She gulps it down and takes him in a bit more, his soft flesh presses against her tongue. Her whole body begins to move as she sucks, her ass lifting a little from the floor with each thrust. The sensation of him sliding from her mouth, then her gently sucking him in again, his wetness dribbling down her chin: all of this makes her dizzy with pleasure. Her fingers knuckle deep in his ass. For a second, she wonders if she is enjoying it too much — if maybe she shouldn't be so aroused by the most vulnerable part of Owen's body. Owen places his hand on the back her head, pulling a hand-ful of hair, and her thoughts of "what if" dissolve.

Through her spread legs, Sherri stares at Owen and he stares back at her. With her feet almost behind her head, her breasts sandwiched tightly between her knees, she drives the vibrator into her pussy. Owen watch-es the gold rod get lost insides folds of pink. Owen loses himself in the slow ooze dripping from her pussy. She makes a series of short squeaking sounds and tosses her head back. "Make some noise for me, baby," she instructs him, and Owen groans along with her, their noises colliding into each other.

"Let's cum at the same time," Sherri says. The vibrator glistens in the candlelight as it darts in and out. Kay moves her tongue around, lapping up his juices. She fills her mouth with him again and sucks faster. Sherri starts an ecstatic mantra of "yes yes yes yes oh yes," as she shakes the vibrator inside her, almost frantic.

Suddenly, what feels like a wall of thick wetness hits Kay's chin and cheeks. Owen flops down on the bed with one final grunt. Kay stretches herself across his groin, covering him, as Sherri gets up, wraps herself in a towel, and goes to leave. "Anytime you want your dick sucked, you come and see us," she says, closing the door behind her.

Kay collapses on the bed beside him. She presses her tongue to the roof of her mouth, wishing she could save this first taste of him in her mouth forever. Her hair is stuck to her face by his cum, her lipstick smeared from nose to chin. Kissing her forehead, he says, "You're a mess."

THE COMING OF YEARS

rp chow

Ellie did not know when it happened. She could not pinpoint the exact second or even duration of transformation — it could have been an infinitesimal shift; it could have transpired within the rushing echo of a single heartbeat. But one night, in the gilt-edged mirror of the bistro washroom, she saw a strange figure gazing curiously back at her. She was not entirely unrecognizable to herself. No, it was more subterranean, as if muscles and bones had shifted beneath her skin.

Even now with her black hair trimmed above her ears and up to the nape of her slender neck, she was less frequently mistaken for a small-framed adolescent boy. Without her noticing, over time her body had settled into fleshy contours. The cyclic rise and fall of estrogen and progesterone through her bloodstream had filled her face with a plump femininity that she had, until recently, failed to detect. Was it simply the accumulation of years that had propelled her body from its gender ambivalence? She had matured into a woman. Aside from the physical, Ellie still wondered if something about her mannerisms or presentation had changed. Why, with the passing of the years, did cashiers and store clerks no longer avoid pronouns when addressing her, but now called her "ma'am" without hesitation?

She continued to peer into the rectangular bathroom mirror. Her eyes were puffy, with laugh lines radiating indiscriminately. Her face assumed various planes, rising and angling in the dim glow of the evening light. Her dimples dug more deeply into her cheeks. When she raised her eyebrows her forehead rippled with creases. When she brushed past girls in nightclubs or at gallery openings, she could discern the under-thirty set:

the strobe lights, the cigarette smoke, and the late hour would sweep cleanly off their smooth, slippery faces. Unlike them, Ellie imagined that her face, with its newly formed ridges and grooves, would bend light and divert rivulets of smoke and sweat. Within the past year, she had acquired texture, like a heavy brush stroke.

In the Hollywood news reports, the newest cosmetic procedure was described as "hand transplants." As the moneyed masses embraced face-lifts, liposuction, and Botox injections, one's physical age was no longer outwardly apparent except for hands whose veins and fine bones pushed against wrinkled, mottled skin. With the cosmetic procedure, collagen was injected to plump up the hands, giving them an almost prepubescent rotundity. Holding up her hands, Ellie studied them closely. She turned the palms down, noting the concentric folds around the finger joints and the blue surfacing of ropey veins. Her hands felt tighter, as if the familiarity of years had pressed her skin more intimately into tendons and cartilage.

"Ellie?" Siu Lin's sleepy voice mumbled from the bedroom.

"In the bathroom," Ellie said, peering out. "I'm coming back."

She bent over and completed her sentence with a flush of the toilet. The pipes clanked in resistance as the tank gurgled its way back to being full. As Ellie straightened up, the pale, round folds of her belly lifted, settled in, then eased into a soft mound. Fine threads of hair fanned out below her once hairless belly button, interlacing gently down to her triangular puff of coarse, black hair. Whose body was this? At certain angles, in various shadows, vestiges of youth shone through: a thigh muscle outlined as she stepped forward, a flow of sinew along her neck as she turned her head, and a ripple of biceps as she stretched canvas onto a frame in her painting studio. We never let go of our youth, she recalled reading in a sociology text: that is why death is always a surprise — the young and the old alike talk about the past, using their memories like a platform from which they leapt into time's currents.

But Ellie marched deliberately into the future, carrying her body safely away from the past. It had nothing to do with historical displacement or a rejection of her roots. Rather, Ellie strove to become the kind of adult who successfully salvages her childhood not by re-entering it, but by letting it rest where it could. Since she was a child, her mind had been weighted by responsibilities. When assigned to do a childhood self-portrait in art college, she had covered the expanse of the page with a large head engulfed by ballooning, sorrowful eyes whose irises swirled inward; this was accompanied by a snub nose, a short scratch of a mouth, and a thin, zigzag neck that connected to a tiny, triangular paisley dress that fell off the bottom right corner of the page.

After she celebrated her thirty-fifth birthday with a bicycle tour through France, Ellie returned home with a sense of confluence, of having finally arrived in her life. Her mind and physical body had negotiated an agreement. Whether her mind had become lighter from the idyllic countryside or her body heavier with contoured cycling muscles, she entrusted her body to the coming years, however numbered they now appeared. It had become easier to count forward instead of backward.

"*Ai-ya!*" Ellie's mother, Cheri Wang, had wailed when Ellie came out to her ten years ago. "*Mut gum gah?*" her mother had waved her arms and gazed imploringly up at the ceiling. When Ellie tried to interject, her mother, as always, beat her to it. "That's enough! I don't want to hear anymore," her mother had said, covering her ears with her hands and walking briskly away.

Now, her mother begrudgingly accepted what she referred to as Ellie's "close friends." Last month, Ellie introduced Siu Lin to her mother. Since Siu Lin looked like Anita Mui, Cheri's favourite Hong Kong movie star, she could not entirely disapprove of Siu Lin. She could only shrug her shoulders and thank the gods that her daughter had good taste in women. If her daughter did not look like Anita Mui, she reasoned, at least she dated someone who did.

If Siu Lin were a few inches taller and a few years younger, Cheri would consider hiring her to model the new fall collection. Her Hong Kong-based label, So Chic, had expanded in the past twenty years due in large part, she felt, to her business acumen and eye for beauty — an eye that her daughter had inherited. Was it Cheri's fault somehow, this gay business of her daughter's? Ellie did grow up surrounded by all manner of beautiful, and often naked, young women when she accompanied Cheri on her shows and buying trips. No, Cheri resolutely and finally decided, appreciating beauty had nothing to do with it, otherwise her models would be running off with each other. No, this gay business was something else.

The first few months were the worst. Cheri would phone Ellie up and demand to know why. Ellie could hear her mother drag unevenly on her cigarette, which meant that she was either nervous or slightly drunk. Ellie felt like a looped synthesized voice, repeating dryly at the end of every phone call: "No, it's not your fault, Mother. No, it's not about you. No, it's not about Father. No, I can't change. I don't want to try. Forget it, then — it *is* your fault. Don't cry, Mother." She would never tell her mother this, but growing up around those beautiful models did give her a then-unidentifiable thrill. They in turn drew her affectionately into their fold, sharing makeup and fashion tips, and kept her company while her mother whisked off to close a deal or finalize production at a factory.

When school was not in session, Ellie would accompany her mother to fashion shows and buying conventions in New York and Paris. One summer in Paris, when Ellie was seventeen, she followed her mother's two favourite models, Remy McLaughlin and Yasmin Wong, to a post-show gala. Remy had enrolled in French classes in Hong Kong, but the rapidity of the spoken language left her smiling vacuously. Yasmin promptly disappeared with her boyfriend. Remy left within the hour, one hand pushing Ellie along ahead of her towards the door as if she were leaving early only on Ellie's behalf. Remy grabbed Ellie's hand as they left the party. They huddled together as they walked, laughing and talking about the other models, about the French they did not comprehend. During their walk back to the hotel, Ellie felt beautiful with Remy as they smiled at passersby. Remy's green eyes were as confident as the sway of her curved body and the tilt of her head as she laughed. That night, Ellie realized what beauty permitted: the ease with which they moved through the Parisian crowd, the smiles lifting like blessings towards them, their flesh warm and alive with the approval of strangers.

At the hotel, they realized their hands were in a sweaty clasp and let go, both wiping hands along dresses and giggling. It was only nine in the evening and Ellie's mother was still out. Remy ran through the suite Ellie shared with her mother, admiring its spaciousness as she brushed her fingers across the furniture and fabric. There were two bedrooms; her mother had always demanded privacy, citing the necessity of creative space. Sometimes she disappeared for weeks when Ellie was in grade school. "Off creating," she would say with a flourish of her hand. Ellie and Remy ordered cream pastries and glasses of cassis from room service.

"Your mother thinks I'm seventeen, but I'm really twenty-one," Remy whispered conspiratorially into Ellie's ear after a few drinks. Her hand pressed lightly then lingered on Ellie's bare arm.

"I'm really seventeen, but my mother thinks I'm twenty-one," Ellie responded, her eyes challenging Remy, as she squeezed then caressed Remy's shoulder through an opening in her dress.

Remy wrinkled her nose and stared at Ellie in silence, gauging the distance between them. Then Remy's lips stretched into a slow smile. She winked and playfully tugged Ellie's arm. "Come," she said. They went into Ellie's bedroom. Ellie stood awkwardly by the window as Remy closed the door and sat on the edge of the bed. In the room with her teddy bear and running shoes, Ellie's stomach tightened as her head expanded with the rush of alcohol. Ellie stared out the window. The brocaded curtains had been pushed open and lights glittered in the distance. Remy turned the lamps off. In the sudden darkness, there was nothing but the pale glow of the Paris skyline. Remy had moved behind Ellie, her breath hot and damp on the back of Ellie's neck. Ellie felt the room expanding, pushing out the window towards the blurred angles of distant buildings shining with tiny lights. She felt a soft burn at the base of her neck, then another and another until Remy's lips spread into a diffuse stream encircling Ellie's neck in blunt waves of heat. "Ssshh," Remy whispered, the palms of her hands pressing Ellie's stiff shoulders in erratic circles. "Ssshh," Remy repeated, her hands sweeping along Ellie's back, around her waist. Ellie felt Remy's breasts press against her shoulder blades. Ellie dropped her gaze from the window and saw Remy's shadowy hands rubbing her stomach in expanding sweeps, then moving up to her breasts. "Ssshh," Remy repeated as Ellie inhaled sharply, her hands clenched. Ellie stood stiffly, wondering at the new weight her breasts assumed in Remy's palms.

When the innumerable coverings of their bodies were finally on the floor, Ellie thought about how, beneath covers, each article presented quiet mysteries to the touch. She had touched her face to the material of

Remy's dress, then her bra, then her underwear, feeling their textures and guessing their patterns in the slow swim towards Remy's skin. Remy had removed Ellie's clothing impatiently, tugging and pulling in jerks as if undressing Ellie for a quick change of outfit at a show.

"What I love about expensive clothes is the way they fall off so smoothly," Remy said, as she rolled and enveloped Ellie with her long body. Ellie held on tightly, her hips following Remy's rhythm. In the thin layer of sweat forming between them, their bodies were yoked as if caught in one another's electromagnetic field, attracted then repelled until their poles spun wildly with new electricity.

A door slammed. "Oh shit," Ellie whispered, arms flailing, trying to twist her body out from beneath Remy. Remy smirked, but didn't release her.

"What time is it?" Ellie asked, peering around the room for her watch. "She won't call me if it's late."

Remy squinted at her watch and asked, "How late is late?"

"After midnight," Ellie said. "If it's after the news broadcast, it's late."

"Then it's late," Remy declared. With a quick squeeze, Remy pulled Ellie's hand under the covers. "I want you inside me."

Remy pressed Ellie's hand down along her stomach, then spread her legs apart and straddled Ellie, pressing heat and liquid into Ellie's thigh as she lifted one leg up to allow Ellie's hand in. Remy moaned. "Yes. Move your fingers around. Here, come inside," Remy sighed, her senses sharpened to a throbbing tip in Ellie's palm. She moved Ellie's hand, directing her with breathy gasps. Remy swayed and twisted, her hands on the pillows beside Ellie, her breasts heaving against Ellie's. Ellie watched Remy's parted lips and closed eyes as her fingers worked in the cramped space. Remy's thighs were clamped around Ellie's knuckles. In the dim light, Ellie watched the small muscles of Remy's face, surprised at the incredible malleability of desire she invoked. "Stop," Remy suddenly commanded, pressing her face into Ellie's neck as her thighs stiffened and her groans slipped further down her throat. Remy loosened and fell heavily against Ellie.

❃

Ellie stole along the hallway of her apartment, squeezing past a purple mountain bike leaning against the shoe rack, then stood quietly at the bedroom doorway. Clothes were strewn about the floor, and the rattan laundry basket overflowed with socks, underwear, and towels. The night table was covered with flyers announcing protest marches, art exhibits, and poetry readings. At the foot of the futon bed, the quilted cotton blanket lay in a lumpy heap, having been kicked aside by restless legs during the night. In the early morning light, Siu Lin's bare shoulders glowed a milky chai brown above the pale blue sheets that had wrapped around her during sleep. Her shoulder-length, copper-streaked hair fell back from her upturned face. For an Asian woman in North America, she was regarded as beautiful: high cheek-bones, long eyelashes, supple breasts, curved hips, and full lips that fixed into a seductive pout. At times, Ellie would surreptitiously stare at her: when Siu Lin bent over her notebook in fierce concentration, seized by a flow of words; when she tossed her head back on the pillows, mouth open and slack in deep sleep; when she closed her eyes during sex, falling deep inside herself as she neared orgasm.

Ellie enjoyed leaving the bed before Siu Lin, so that she could return to find her wrapped in sheets like a dreamy surprise. Siu Lin was Ellie's Goldilocks, a beautiful young thing who stole into her home and fell asleep in her bed. Eight years younger than Ellie, Siu Lin seemed so confident, so certain of her place in Ellie's life. "Hey, sweetie," Siu Lin had smiled one morning early on in their undefined amorphous coupling, throwing her arm around Ellie and claiming her with two simple words. By contrast, Ellie's image of Siu Lin vacillated. She saw Siu Lin as a landed immigrant in the weathered country of her flesh. Without citizenship, Siu Lin could leave without notice, and Ellie could absolve herself of any obligations and believe her skin could, at will, remove any traces of Siu Lin.

In the past few months, Ellie found herself unsettled by once familiar matters. This uncertainty originated within her changing body, and seeped into her external surroundings. In the studio, her old paintings huddled in forgotten shapes behind ragged pieces of cloth; when unveiled, their colours burst raucously like loud, nervous strangers in a quiet room: stark blues, rusted reds, and even the browns and blacks struck a sharper visual force. Now, the measured rise and fall of Siu Lin's breasts and belly made Ellie feel like an intruder in her own bedroom. Her gangly limbs and angular torso felt out of place.

Siu Lin twitched awake with a sudden, soft snort. "Hey, baby, I can't believe I fell asleep again. How long have you been standing there?"

"Not long."

Siu Lin's voice penetrated Ellie's watchful solitude. Sitting on the edge of the futon, Ellie leaned down and kissed Siu Lin's nose, smelling her sleepy parts: tousled hair, dry mouth, sweat-laced neck.

"Mmm, I had the wildest dream," Siu Lin said. "You were this hot chick I was trying to pick up at a conference. You were leading a workshop on women and casual sex. All the women I've had sex with were there, plus all the women I wanted to avoid. Then we were alone in your room. I got up to lock the door, but the door didn't fit the frame, so I had to push it and angle it in. You sucked my breasts through my T-shirt. Then we were at another workshop and you wouldn't talk to me! Said you didn't talk to anyone you'd had sex with, which pissed me off so much that I woke up."

Siu Lin threw her arms up around Ellie's neck and laughed at her dream. "I had the most amazing sleep, though." She stretched like a contented cat. Her breasts and one leg pushed out from the tangle of sheets. With outstretched arms, she tilted towards Ellie and pressed her soft, pale nipples against Ellie's cool, bare stomach. "Ooh, you're so cold, you're giving me goosebumps!"

"And you're so hot, you're turning me on," Ellie said.

"Am I?" Siu Lin pulled back and raised herself up on her elbow, tossing back her long, layered hair. "I thought you were looking introspective."

"What do you mean?"

"Ellie, whenever you get that faraway look, whenever you're watching me as if from another galaxy, I know you're checking me out. Like you're thinking me through before you touch."

"What? I don't do that. You make me sound like a repressed academic."

"But Ellie, the more you theorize, the more you want to practice. Or maybe it's not theorizing; maybe you're setting me up, composing me."

"No," Ellie said, but her protest was weak. She squinted at Siu Lin's body, seeing her as a charcoal sketch: a visualization of light and shadows, innocent of colours.

"Face it, sweetie," Siu Lin said, "you fuck like you paint. You see me, then you see the me you want to paint."

Siu Lin did not have Ellie's perceptive eye for outline and detail. The more Siu Lin looked at someone, the less she saw and the less she recalled. She could discern strangers, but lovers eluded her. There were so many details to a lover's body, modulated by vocal tones, moods, and facial expressions, that Siu Lin could not keep track of the intricacies of intimacy. How did Ellie see her? What did she focus on?

"No," Ellie paused, carefully weighing her words. "I only see the person that you want me to see."

"I don't think I can change the way you see anything. Especially me."

Ellie laughed uneasily. Although she had sketched and painted friends and other lovers, she had never asked Siu Lin to model for her. When Siu Lin saw those paintings and ink sketches, she had turned questioningly to Ellie, but remained silent. Before Ellie could respond, Siu Lin had looked away and the moment passed. "If a woman poses for you, she gives herself to you," Ellie recalled Modigliani's words. Ellie did not want to possess anyone, not at this stage in her life when she could barely account for herself. Through the wooden slats of the window blinds, streaks of sunlight sharpened against Siu Lin's skin. Ellie hovered over Siu Lin's lowered head, kissed her tousled hair, then licked the slivers of light that had cut across Siu Lin's face and shoulders.

"Mmm, what do you see now?" Siu Lin licked Ellie's dark nipple with a swift flick of her tongue and giggled, turning away to expose her bare back down to the base of the spine at the cleft between her round buttocks. She tilted her head invitingly, brushing hair aside to reveal the flowing curve of her neck.

Siu Lin's neck tasted mildly salty to Ellie's dry tongue. Ellie licked her lips, and then pressed her nose and mouth into the warm hollow below Siu Lin's jaw. Her hand smoothed the sheets down to Siu Lin's rounded hips, then she drew her fingers down Siu Lin's back to the base of her spine. Ellie then retraced the path of her hand with her tongue. Siu Lin's low sighs broke wordless joust of tongue and saliva against the arc of skin and its slick layer of anticipation. Siu Lin lay still, then turned onto her stomach as if on command as Ellie's fingers fanned across her ass cheeks before slipping into the crevice. Ellie's tongue arrived seconds later and dipped in as her hands pressed against Siu Lin's cheeks; she spread them roughly, then eased them gently back.

"Your tongue's an awesome afterthought. Or are your fingers just the opening act?" Siu Lin murmured into the pillows. "So, are you still sketching me with your tongue?"

"No, I'm colouring you in."

Siu Lin gasped as Ellie's tongue lay flat and heavy upon the skin that overlay the tendon that stretched between her anus and vagina. Ellie tongued towards Siu Lin's warm, damp undulations; she stroked in straight lines, then rubbed in shadows. Siu Lin's hips rose and fell, guiding Ellie closer and deeper, her ass cheeks widening, then clamping tight. Kneeling at the edge of the low futon, Ellie leaned into Siu Lin's gyrating thrusts, her breaths pulled into all of Siu Lin's openings. Ellie lifted her head up to catch her breath. Siu Lin drew her legs up, shifted her weight to her knees, and pushed her ass up. She slowly rocked her hips, spreading with each upward sway. Kneeling at the foot of the futon, Ellie gazed at the fragrant offering. The smell of slumber between Siu Lin's legs filled Ellie's nostrils: hot, ripe, and nocturnal. With each eager thrust of her hips, Siu Lin's deep red lips spread. Her anus puckered in the rhythmic rocking. Ellie flattened then sharpened her tongue against the tight circumference, licking the edges and then darting in as the sphincter gradually relaxed with each of Siu Lin's moans.

Was it Siu Lin who caused her to be analytical during sex, or had she always been like this? Shifting in and out of her body, as if she could inhabit or abandon herself at will? Who is this beautiful woman with her face buried in that groaning woman's ass? Who is that beautiful woman, hair falling forward onto pillows, now up on all fours, her back arching with aching need? Siu Lin, with her fleshy curves and electric blue nails, with hair bands and yoga tights. Siu Lin, wriggling in tight dresses with a deep cleavage. Siu Lin, who inhabited her womanhood with seemingly effortless skill and panache. Siu Lin, who knew what she wanted when she wanted it, who was now urgently pushing her hungry ass towards Ellie's face.

"You feel so good," Siu Lin growled. "I can't bear it." With a quick tilt of her hips, Siu Lin pulled her ass back and down, swung around, and grabbed Ellie's face with her hands. Her kiss swallowed Ellie's lips as her arms dragged Ellie up and onto the bed until their legs were entwined and their nipples grazed then met in a tight press. Crushed against Siu Lin, Ellie brushed back Siu Lin's tangle of hair. Pushing herself backwards along the sheets, Siu Lin lowered her right arm into the emerging space between their open and entwined legs. Her palm pressed into Ellie's erect clit as her fingers slid along and around the warm cushion of hair. Siu Lin withdrew her tongue as Ellie's breaths quickened and her head tilted back. Siu Lin sucked and gnawed at Ellie's neck. Her fingers traced the tip of Ellie's stiff clit, then stroked downward along the edges and ripples, circling the slippery ridges, until one of her fingers slipped in.

"Fuck me." Ellie moaned, leaned back against the wall, and raised one bent leg until her ankle rested on Siu Lin's shoulder.

"Sure you're wet enough? Open enough?"

Siu Lin roughly rubbed her knuckles up and down Ellie's clit until her fingers were hot and sticky. With her free left hand, she grabbed Ellie's right hand and pulled it down toward her own slippery cunt. She lifted her knees and stretched her thighs widely into a lotus position. Ellie's palm pressed into Siu Lin's exposed and throbbing mound. Siu Lin's hair was matted, damp, and slick.

"Your fingers are sweet and hot: caramel swirled on vanilla ice cream. You're cottony warm: sunset orange turned inside out," Ellie whispered as she licked Siu Lin's earlobe.

Siu Lin eased one finger in and probed the heat as juices made her fingers slide and slip.

"Umm, babe, getting wetter and wider."

With her right hand, Ellie guided Siu Lin's left hand between their exposed cunts and held one finger of Siu Lin's in her hand and used it to touch Siu Lin along her hard clit. With the fingers of her left hand, Ellie pushed against the soft wet of Siu Lin's opening. Together, they fingered Siu Lin's thrusting pussy. Siu Lin stretched her mouth into a perfect O. She tilted forward and grazed her hair along Ellie's breasts, which sloped into hardened nipples. As Siu Lin rocked her hips, her deep breaths filled the room. Sweat glistened between her breasts as she fell back into the pillows.

Ellie stroked Siu Lin's thighs as she quietly listened to Siu Lin's ragged breaths grow steadily softer and more even.

"Hey, sweetie," Siu Lin said, offering Ellie a lop-sided grin. She sat up again and wet her fingers with lube. She parted Ellie's lips and rubbed the edges of her pussy, then slid her thumb across Ellie's throbbing clit. All she could feel was all the disparate parts of her life coming together in Siu Lin's hands.

THE SCENE HERE SUCKS:
A Lurid Tale of Innocence Lost

Elaine Miller

I'm hungry. No. That isn't strong enough. I'm starved; hurtingly so. And I'm not altogether sure that I might find proper sustenance in this awful neighbourhood. A month ago, I would have been frightened to stray from Father's protective arm and walk these streets alone. A month ago, when I was this hungry, I might have said aloud, the Lord will provide. Now I'm not sure if I'm allowed to ask for help from that direction any more.

Even now, at what must be close to midnight, the grime and garbage on the street are obvious under the unfamiliar glare of electric lights. The sheer number of people is shocking. I don't know why they don't go to their homes. Maybe they don't have homes. In my little town in Pennsylvania, Father orders vagrants to be shunned. Everybody listens to Father, because he's the Elder. Or — was the Elder.

"Daughter," he'd say, right up until last month, "people who are not evil-eschewing, properly baptized Christians don't belong in the same town as people like you and me."

I used to belong in that town. That sweet little place where the streets are clean and quiet, and all the hardworking farm people stay indoors after dark, sleeping or reading the bible by candlelight, especially on Saturday nights, because everyone goes to church on Sunday morning.

The only people you'd find out-of-doors are the nasty ones, like some of those unmarried young people, sneaking away to roll around and do sinful things in barns. I remember the couple I stumbled upon three weeks ago, Mary King and Amos Fisher, and my stomach rumbles noisily. They were doubly sinful because Amos was secretly stepping out on his betrothed, which purely is not right. I sucked them dry with a certain feeling of righteousness.

But that night three weeks ago was the last time I ate. Tonight, I study the people around me. I'd like to eat one, but they smell wrong, especially the ones who shout blasphemy into the air. I suspect some of them might be junkers, or dope addicts, or whatever they're called.

I smooth the long folds of my black dress — the one I wore to Father's funeral and that I've been wearing ever since — down my legs and wish that Father hadn't gotten himself eaten, because he would be able to tell me what to do. He always could.

The monster — I think I'm supposed to call her Master, since she ate Father she made me into what I am now. She stuffed me in a shipping crate the night after I ate Mary and Amos. She said a great deal of rude and scathing things, that killing without hiding the cause of death was defecating in one's own nest, endangering others of our kind. Except she didn't say "defecate." She said she'd tried to teach me what I was and how I must behave, but that I hadn't listened. She said that she should have known that turning out a religious zealot would be a bad idea. She was mad.

Then the Master put me in my crate and loaded it on the bottom of a stack of similar crates into a boxcar on a train bound for Canada. I couldn't turn to mist and escape, because there were too many crates around me to seep through them all. I'd risk complete dissolution. I think she knew how long it would take for the train to reach its destination, and I don't think she cared.

So, after three weeks in the crate, I am weak. And I'm hungry. My waist-length black hair has come undone from its bun, and my headcovering is long gone. I'm also afraid that I look like anyone else on these awful streets: shuffling along, clutching my belly and half-bent over with a sharp, craving need etched on my face.

I walk for a while; the streets seem cleaner, less threatening. That's a relief, although I avert my eyes from the heavily made-up women standing on the street corners with their short skirts hiked up and their bosoms on display. They don't smell like food either, having that poison taint of ill-health. Father and the rest of the church elders didn't allow such loose women on the streets back home.

I turn a corner and find the front door of a bar where a lot of people are standing outside, smoking and talking. Excited by the idea of someone to eat, I push past the crowd into a narrow, grubby hallway. When the woman at the door puts out an arm to block my path and looks like she may demand something of me, I *bewilder* her with some effort. She obediently removes her arm, and I step inside.

I stop just inside the entrance, awash in dreadful, cacophonous music, breathing in the warm scent of so many bodies crammed, all of them dancing and sweating, into such a small space. There's something odd about this scene, though. They are all women. Some are immodestly dressed hussies with kohl-blackened eyes, and others (at first glance, male) are short-haired women dressed like tradesmen in low-slung jeans and tight men's T-shirts. All of these women are dancing with each other, I suppose because there are no men around. Where are their husbands and betrotheds?

I move through the room, looking for one I can eat. I was counting on finding a man because I think I could lure one away from the crowd by pretending to be helpless. I wonder how on earth I might persuade one of these women to follow me away from this place. I will have to do this carefully, and plan how I will feed, because I can never think clearly when my eye teeth grow long and sharp. All I can feel at such times is the lust for feeding.

Then the thought is torn from my spinning head by the most exciting scent in the world. Someone here is bleeding. I follow the scent to a closed, unmarked door near the back of the bar, and under the pounding music, I hear faint cries of suffering — just as I used to salivate as Mother ladled stew onto my plate, I feel an ache in my eye teeth, a feeling of imminent pleasure.

I gently try the doorknob, which refuses to turn. Locked. But praise Jesu — thankfully, there's another way, even if it costs me in reserves of strength. Not wishing to be seen, I cast a net of *bewilderment* as far as I can, and with a tremendous effort, I change to mist and seep under the door.

Reforming slowly inside, dismayed at my sudden weakness, the blood-scent strikes me like a physical blow, and I nearly lose my ever-loving mind. The *bewildering* I cast has made me invisible to those in the room with me, so I look around carefully. What on God's green earth, what in hell is happening here?

I am in a warm, cozy room with soft lighting. The pervasive beat of the ear-cracking music in the club is much quieter here, making a heartbeat for the room. A selection of odd-looking furniture is scattered about, and in the centre of the room, a small crowd of women is gathered around one who is squealing, bleeding and naked. Many are those strange masculine women, but these seem to be motorcycle riders, judging by their leather attire. Presiding over everything is a tall, strong-looking woman dressed almost like the whores outside, except she shows much more skin, and her carriage is that of a queen, sure and proud.

They're torturing the naked woman, pushing thin steel needles into her skin. But no, that's not quite right. I take a second look. The soft, pale, and extremely curvy woman in the centre with her long hair pulled up into a ponytail looks like she's enjoying it. She smiles up at the women as they take their turns, their gloved hands carefully pushing needle after needle just under her skin, then pulling them back out again. When each sharp point pierces her, she quietly whimpers but continues to smile.

The feminine woman who seems to be directing this strange little scene glances at me for a moment. Hurriedly, I *bewilder* her. She shakes her head and then focuses on me more sharply than before. Why is she strong enough to see me? Her obvious mental struggle catches the attention of the others, and their combined focus is too much for me to withstand. I'm fully visible.

"Some wacked-out goth chick," one says.

"Bugger off. This is a private party," says another.

At a loss for words, I gesture helplessly to the thin streaks of blood on the plump woman's body, and I wonder how I will get what I need. Then what's left of my self-control lapses entirely. They are locked in this room with me — I'll just eat them all, starting with the one who smells so good.

I leap towards the bleeding woman, letting out my inner monster. My hands stretch into claws, the tendons standing out in sharp relief, and my eye teeth spring from my upper jaw. I ignore everyone except my intended. They'll start screaming and running, I know from experience. She is within my grasp, her pleasure-glazed eyes startled but unafraid.

But then suddenly, it feels like every woman in the room has her rough hands on me.

"Whoa!" they shout. They're angry; they slam me face down on the floor as my woman staggers back, protective of her naked, pierced body. Dimly, in my bloodrage I sense that there's something wrong. None of them screamed, none of them ran away.

"Evette, are you all right?" someone asks.

"Fucking newbie," someone else yells at me. "You negotiate, stupid bitch, you don't touch someone in scene."

My monster still controls me, and unthinking, I roar and struggle. I must have the blood! But too many strong arms hold me back.

"Catch her arm! Now the other one!" There is a metallic ratcheting noise. "You got her feet? Fuck, she's trying to bite me. Hand me the — yeah, thanks."

The use of my hands and feet have been taken somehow, and I'm lashing out with the only weapon I've got left. Mid-snap, a hard rubber bit is thrust between my molars, behind my fangs, and its straps are secured snugly behind my head. The kiss of steel hardware on my cheeks from this dreadful apparatus pulls me back to reality. My inner monster abruptly deserts me and I can begin to think clearly once more. I could weep.

A moment more, and with the slithering sound of rope, my ankles are drawn up to meet my wrists behind my back, and I am helpless on the floor. The women all begin talking at once.

"Get the bouncer. Let's get this fucking gothling out of here."

"Where'd she come from?"

"Look, we must have knocked her fake fangs off. Are they on the floor anywhere?"

"What was that all about? This chick is nuts."

"C'mon, let's drag her out to the front door, and call the police to come get her."

"No." This from Evette. "Anybody wants something that bad, maybe they should get a taste of it." This gains her some sharp looks, while others laugh.

"No, seriously," she continues. "When I first found out about the scene, I needed to bottom so bad it nearly killed me. I'm sure I might have done the same thing if I found myself in her shoes, watching us play. I'll bet she's never seen anything like this in her life. Ain't that right, girlie?"

I nod absently, desperately trying to find a framework for this language. Scene? Bottom? Play? All I understand is that my strength is nearly gone. Certainly I can't mist again without feeding. If I'm given to the authorities in this city I'll be found out, or at best, locked overnight in a cell, where the daylight may come and kill me. I am completely at their mercy.

"C'mon, Ramona," says Evette, smiling up at the tall, feminine woman. "Let's let her play too."

Ramona nears, and at her approval, I'm hauled up onto my knees by some of the other women, my arms and legs still bound. One of them gently unbuckles the straps holding the rubber bit in place in my mouth, and drops it to the floor. Ramona leans over, her long hair falling forward and brushing against my skin, and places her hands on either side of my face in a not unkindly way.

"Do you really want to be in this scene? Or shall we take you out and let you go?" she asks.

Her wise eyes have smoky black lashes, and her lips gleam dark and red. Perhaps she's a succubus, created solely to capture souls with her wanton sexuality. I try to answer, but the thud of her pulse in her wrists is too close, too tempting, and I lose control and snap sideways at one of her hands.

Ramona slaps me casually. "Evette isn't often wrong about people," she smiles. "Last chance. Do you need this? Do you want to play with us?"

Shocked at the slap, my cheek stinging, I stare into her eyes and over-will her. At least I try to, but she shrugs off the attempt with only a slight frown to show she's noticed. Evette comes close, the scent of her sweet blood on her skin beyond intoxicating. I close my eyes briefly, the hunger an agony. A strange desire to please washes over me.

"Yes, ma'am," I say, my voice weak from long disuse. "Yes, I'd like to be part of what you're doing here. Please."

"What's your name, sweetheart?" asks Evette, who is leaning close, far too close.

"Faith," I say carefully, having thought, after last month, to never say the name again.

"My name is Faith."

I look at Evette, excitement flushing her face and the tops of her breasts. It's her blood I want, more than anything I've ever wanted in either my life or my death. All I can think of is her blood, drying on her skin or fresh and wet around the tiny steel needles.

"Your safeword," says Ramona, looking me firmly in the eye, "is '*red*'."

Somehow I barely notice they've unbuttoned my black dress and peeled it down to my waist. They fasten me into a piece of furniture that I recognize from our history books. Except I don't think those stocks were ever carefully padded, nor would they have had pretty brass clips holding them closed.

Then another padded apparatus, something between a stepstool and a sawhorse, is dragged in front of me. Evette places a sheet over it like a housewife covering her good couch. She steps onto it carefully, minding her needles, as she kneels on the lower step, and leans over the upper. We're face to face now, as close as a married couple in the privacy of their bedroom.

"Remember, honey, if you need anything to stop, or get freaked out, you say your safeword, and we stop and let you go. Got that?"

I nod, speechless.

The mood of the room shifts, heating up in an inexplicable way. I spot two women by the door kissing and holding one another, another pair pulling coiled ropes out of a bag, and one woman picking up an object that I recognize an object that I recognize from the history books as a cat o' nine tails. She approaches me, smiling.

At the first slap of the whip, I jump, having steeled myself for terrible pain. But it doesn't really hurt. As the next blow falls and the next, a warmth begins to spread across my shoulders. It barely distracts me from watching what else is happening in the room.

Ramona opens her bag and pulls out a long, thick, purple object, which she places in some kind of harness. Then she pulls up her short skirt and tugs the contraption on like bloomers. The purple object protrudes outward and upward from her crotch; it's shaped like the medical illustrations I've seen of a man's penis, only bigger.

It turns out, despite what I've become, that I can blush after all.

Evette smiles broadly at Ramona, wiggling her full buttocks. "Oh yeah," she says. "I hope that's for me."

Ramona grins at her. "Yeah, you should know — since you packed the bag, you salacious slut."

Evette smiles happily at this shocking insult, so I add this word "slut" to the new list of terms that seem to have a different meaning in this place. The woman behind me continues to thump my shoulders with the whip, which feels oddly relaxing. My lust — for blood, of course — is making everything seem surreal, so I'm not even surprised when Ramona, after a passionate kiss with Evette, moves behind her and douses her purple object with a thick liquid from a small bottle. Although I can't see precisely what happens, she does something that makes Evette catch her breath and hold it, waiting. Over the gentle slapping sound of the whip that warms my back, I hear Ramona whisper, "We're gonna go real slow, baby. I know you're craving it hard, so I'm gonna do it easy."

Evette whimpers in a frustrated kind of way, then opens her eyes wide and moans in my direction as Ramona grasps her hips in a pleased and proprietary way and leans into her. Now maybe I don't have any experience with this sort of thing at all, but I can picture what's happening here, and the warmth from the whip moves down from my shoulders. It makes me feel strangely funny, like the bloodthirst, only different.

We do this for a long time, slow like Ramona promised, as she pushes and pulls gently with her hips, each stroke taking forever. Evette moans softly, more flushed than before with all that delicious blood. Her whole body moves with Ramona; her face is close enough to kiss me, and she almost lets it happen, her lips brushing mine again and again. I want her to kiss me, I think because then I could bite her.

The woman behind me strokes my skin with the whip, then her hand, then the whip again, laying a steady succession of thumps across my back. My skin feels hot and tight and itchy; each smack of the whip scratches me. I'd allowed this game so I could get a chance at eating Evette. But it feels so good. I want to keep feeling it. For the first time since even before I died, I feel alive.

And still, I'm so very hungry. And Evette smells better and better as she moans and twists and sweats on Ramona's purple rod.

I bend the last shreds of my will to *bewilder* Evette. I look deep into her eyes, willing her closer. As she gazes at my face, her brow creased with sudden tension, my fangs slide out to their full length, exposing the depth of my need. For a moment she looks startled, but then she smiles.

"Oh honey, I can't be compelled by you, or anyone," she says softly, just to me. "But that thing you do with the fangs — now that's really, really kinky. I know what you want. And I'm willing to give it to you."

With a sharp gasp, Evette pulls three needles from her right nipple, starting the blood flowing once more. She shifts forward without losing Ramona, cups her heavy breast in one hand, and offers her nipple to me, sliding it neatly between my fangs and into my wet mouth.

Gratefully I suckle, pulling the first few drops of her warm life's blood slowly through the tiny holes in her skin, imbibing strength and vitality with each swallow. The taste of this, the first freely-given blood I've ever had, burns through me like fire and is far more potent than anything I've experienced.

I suppose I could have more blood by tearing at Evette's soft nurturing breast with my fangs. Instead, I accept her trust, and take only what she offers so freely. Encouraged by her moans, I suck harder, rasping the surface of Evette's nipple with my eager tongue, aware of the stiffness of the raspberry-sized nub.

I can't see and I can't think; all I'm aware of is Evette, her breasts full of sweet, freely offered blood, and the roaring noise in my ears. Then Ramona's constant purr changes to a growl, and Evette's constant soft gasps change to cries as Ramona's thrusts push her into my face.

The nipple in my mouth is suddenly whisked away, leaving me open-mouthed and begging. Evette, her face blurry from pleasure, slides the needles from her left breast with a groan, and then pushes it into my mouth. Her nipple drips its scorching hot blood on my tongue.

We're all moving faster, bouncing around, and it's hard to keep suckling. Careful not to slice her breast with my fangs, I suck powerfully, pulling strongly, determined to keep it at all costs. Evette's muscles start to tense, and as a dim part of me that's not occupied with ecstatic feeding wonders what's happening, she starts saying under her breath, over her shoulder, "Yeah, harder, oh, please." And I guess Ramona agrees, because she starts shoving herself into Evette who howls encouragement.

I'm blinded by Evette's breast and deafened by the wet sound of their bodies slapping together. The burn from the whip has spread through me, and there's good blood in my mouth. I've never been happier. But then Ramona starts to shout hoarsely, and Evette, who has been coiling like a spring, decides to let all that go at just that instant.

Evette screams, loud and long, and a feeling I've never experienced blasts through me. I open my mouth to scream. The last drops of blood on my tongue ignite a fire through my body and brain, and I *feel* all three of us explode inside my mind.

For a moment, I *am* Ramona, buried inside Evette, and I *am* Evette, with her quirky, incredible capacity for taking pleasure and pain. And, finally, I *am* myself; the monster I've become, merged with the girl I was. My mind's fully opened now, and I understand far more than I did as either the girl or the demon.

I'm Faith. And I have a bright new future.

EDGE PLAY

Daphne Gottlieb

> *Fact and fiction have furnished many extraordinary examples of crime that have shocked the feelings and staggered the reason of men, but I think no one of them has ever surpassed in its mystery the case that you are now considering.*
>
> —George Robinson, Lizzie Borden's defence lawyer

> *I must be cruel, only to be kind: Thus bad begins and worse remains behind.*
>
> —William Shakespeare

Borden has secrets, locked tight in her body, just under her skin. When I trail my fingertips over the tops of her forearms, just gently brushing them, I can feel them swarm up, closer, like goldfish at feeding time.

You can break girls by knowing their secrets, using their secrets to pry them apart and watch their succulent hearts beating, vulnerable, slick. Most girls I know, in their secret heads, want to be told how dirty they are. *Such a good little slut. Spread your little whore legs for me, you cunt. You like that, don't you.* They twitch and glisten, swell, gasp and moan, and push up. They're aching and desperate for the touch that lets them prove what shameless hussies, what brazen fucks, they are. So many girls with the same secret.

Not Borden. Borden's secrets smell like blood. Tonight, she comes to me and kneels in front of me, eyes down. *Look at me, Borden,* I tell her. She doesn't. She is waiting, eyes screwed tight, chin down, for the sting of my palm against her cheek. I've got something else in mind for her tonight. I've seen her at parties, beaten and flogged until her skin turned pink, red, purple and the once-eager tops were exhausted and frustrated; watched her back cut into latticework until it wept blood. I've seen her take fists and dildos roughly. She never tears up, she never breaks.

Borden, I say quietly, not touching her. I crouch down next to her and she stiffens. I take the back of her collar in my hand and she braces, waiting for it to tighten against her throat. Instead, I slip the leather back through its buckle, slide it apart, roll it up, and put it aside, next to us on the floor. Her hands fly to her throat; her eyes open wide. I take her hands in mine and run my fingers over hers, gently. Cupping her chin in my palm, I look at her. *Borden, you are such a pretty girl*, I tell her. *I'm so lucky to be with you.* I help her to stand and we walk over to her couch. I run my hand over her hair, gently, careful not to snag a single strand, telling her how wonderful she is. *I'm so lucky to be here with you*, I say, and her lower lip starts to tremble. Her eyes well up and threaten tears.

I tell her she's precious so she blushes and burns with shame. And when I stroke her tenderly, she winces and shudders, ashamed and terrified and craving more. And so I kiss her with the tiniest busses, the mouth's smallest hints, ocean mist over her ears, throat, cheeks. She's pushing against me with the ardour of a teenager even though she's pushing four decades. *Oh, not yet, Borden, I want this to last, to last....* and my hands trail down over her shirt, carefully avoiding the nipples that are straining against the fabric. I stroke the backs of her knees, graze slowly over the tops of her thighs just where her skirt ends, and she pulls me down against her, roughly. *Please*, she says. *Please, oh* — her breath is hot and fast and her voice is choked by want. Urgent.

She's shaking, wanting me to stop and never wanting me to, but I want more. I want to see her split apart by flesh and heat. I want to see her in abandon. In the throes of this desire, Borden becomes all hands. And those hands have only one thing to do: grab for the axe.

I whisper her name in her ear. Not the one she's told me to call her. *Elizabeth*, I say. *Oh, my Lizzie* — and she howls and bucks against me, and fills the room with her raw-throated cries. There's no axe in sight. She's got me between her palms. And I shine deadly sharp.

CLEAN PANTIES

Ducky DooLittle

I was delighted to find a laundromat that stayed open so late. The miserable washing machine in my apartment building was on the fritz again and me being a night owl, it was getting more and more difficult to get this task done. I have enough panties and socks and all to last at least a week and a half, but this night I was desperate; I was down to my last pair of panties and had worn them for two days. I'm healthy and my pussy is fragrant, but not dirty. I always change my panties, but like I said, on this night I was desperate.

So I showed up with two bags of dirty laundry, hair piled on top of my head and feeling rather frightful. I had thrown on a pair of sling-back heels and a sweater that matched my skirt. I looked at my reflection in the glass door and thought this wasn't exactly the kind of thing most people would wear to the laundromat. I just didn't have time to think about what I was wearing and most of my favorite things were in these bags. And anyway, there was just one other person in the laundromat besides me.

He looked kind of bored and was entertaining himself by reading a magazine. But after setting my things down, I could tell he was just using it as a prop to look busy. He was watching me do my laundry. He must be really bored, I thought.

I started to load up the machine. I am not terribly domesticated. As I almost finished stuffing my things in, half of them came tumbling back out at my feet. It seemed to me as though they should have fit! He saw me struggling and said I was trying to fit too much in one washer.

"What are you? The freaking laundry attendant?" I said, frustrated.

"As matter a fact, I am. And if you put too much clothing in one load, your clothes won't get clean. Trust me. I do this every day."

I was a little embarrassed. I didn't realize it was his job to watch me. I apologized and took his advice. After all, he was just doing his job. He looked to be about thirty years old and not a bad-looking guy. I kind of wondered why a man would be a laundry attendant. It's a weird job.

"Oh, and by the way, the change machine is out of order," he added. "If you need quarters, you'll have to go to the grocery store on the corner."

I grabbed my purse and darted off to the store. As I was came back into the Laundromat, I saw the guy rummaging around in one of my machines. I startled him as I approached. He looked a little sweaty and made some excuse about trying to help me. He said he was rearranging the clothes so that they would fit in the washer better. Now, that was being a little too helpful, don't you think? As he was stammering to make up his excuse, I could see the lacy trim of a pair of my panties sticking out of his pocket. He also had an erection that he could not hide. His cock was about to burst through his pants. Did he think I was stupid?

I kept my eyes on him as I started to put quarters in the machine. He looked down and pushed his hand deep in his pocket, trying to hide his crime. He turned and walked back to his seat. As I started up the machines, I thought of a great way to pass the time waiting for them to finish.

I went up to him and asked him, quite innocently, "What time do you stop letting people wash clothes? When is the last wash?"

"Ten p.m.," he answered.

"I see. I want you to know that I saw you steal my panties. I know they're in your pocket right now. It is a quarter past ten now; I expect you to lock the door and get your ass back here or I swear I'll tell your boss what you've done and have you fired."

Oh, the look of fear on his face — I had him right where I wanted him and was getting such a thrill out of pushing this panty thief around.

He locked the door and raced back. I could see his erection was once again straining in his pants. I told him to lay down on the floor with his hands at his side, which he did immediately, his wide eyes staring up at me. "What is it that you were planning on doing with those panties of mine?" I asked.

"I smell them. I wanted to jerk off in them," he said hesitantly.

I placed my foot on his cock and applied some pressure. I could feel how hard he was. I wished I could feel his pulsating hard-on with my toes, but my shoes were a better implement for torturing a thief right now. I saw his eyes dart straight up my skirt. This had to be almost painful, the way he wanted to smell my pussy juices. I'm sure there had to be a wet spot blatantly displaying my excitement too.

I enunciated each word with a little pressure from my foot as I told him, "Take the panties out of your pocket and show me how you jerk off in them!" Then I pushed off with my foot.

He unbuttoned his pants and reached down inside the band of his boxers, and his engorged cock sprang forward and up towards his belly button. He reached into his pocket and took out the panties. He took his cock in one hand as he held the panties up with the other. His eyes broke contact with me as he looked at my dainty panties. He put his cock through one of the leg holes so that the crotch panel wrapped completely around his cock. Then he wrapped his fist around the panties and began stoking himself.

His graceful stokes and his method of wrapping the panties around his cock made it obvious that he was a seasoned panty thief. As I watched him jerking himself off, I could feel my panties getting sopping wet. I stepped over him so that I was straddling his body. I lifted my skirt and started to touch my clit. My panties were dripping and I just had to cum. But I was going to be damned if he got to cum before me, so I knelt down with a knee on either side of his head and forced my pelvis down hard on his face. After all, he was the one who had something to lose here, he was the one who should suffer, so I felt like I didn't need to hold back. He should pay me for those panties, and pay me in orgasms.

I tugged at the panties with one hand, using the other to keep my balance as I felt myself losing control. My pussy lips were peeking out of either side of the panties I was wearing. He was working my hot twat with his mouth and tongue. As he sucked my juices through the fabric, I lost my breath and pushed my pussy down on his face and came hard with multiple tremors. I was exhausted.

I fell forward and rested my head on my arms, my panty-clad ass still hovering over his face. I looked under me to see him still jerking off wildly and smelling the fragrant panties I was wearing. Then, with that same seasoned grace, he came just as hard as me and used my panties to sop up the heavy load of jizz.

As he lay there trying to catch his breath, I could hear the spin cycle of my washing machines come to a halt. I didn't even have to ask him to put my things in the dryer; he just got up and did it.

When he returned, I was sitting in a chair with my legs spread, wet panties dangling off my foot. I had stripped them off and was leisurely touching my pussy. He got down on his knees and began to lick it with long, slow strokes. I could feel the momentum returning as I began to push my pelvis out to meet his tongue. This continued until I came in his face again.

As I put on a fresh pair of panties hot from the dryer, I looked up at the wall and saw the laundromat's business license. Sure enough, this guy was not the attendant; he was the owner. He never had a fear of getting fired. He had a big smile on his face as I picked up my bags of clean clothes and headed home. A few days later, they fixed the machine in my building, so I've never had to return to that laundromat. But maybe I will some day, if I think my panties need more than a wash.

KNIFED

Sherece Taffe

Tienne and Dianne had gone to bed angry. They loved each other fierce-ly, but fought passionately and often. This time, they argued about the amount of time that Tienne spent doing things she claimed she did not want to do. Dianne thought that if she would just get into the habit of not taking on other people's shit, Tienne would be better able to set and maintain boundaries. The morning allowed a clearer perspective for both women as they spent many hours making up and fucking. Their lovemak-ing was rough and wild and exhausting.

Tienne hums as she leaves for her morning walk. Nearing the park, she is in such a reverie that she doesn't hear Dianne as she approaches from behind. In fact, she doesn't hear anything until Dianne puts a hand over her mouth and whispers in her ear, "Don't make a sound and you won't get hurt." Tienne feels a rushing warmth between her legs as a blade touches the skin on the back of her neck. It is cool and hard and sharp. With each intake of air, she can feel the knife threatening her flesh.

"Keep walking and keep silent." Dianne fears for a moment that the scene won't work in quite so public a venue. She fears that someone will witness them and try to aid Tienne. She fears that Tienne will decide not to consent to an unplanned public encounter. But mostly, Dianne fears that she will really have to do what she has set out to do. How can she imagine that she can fuck Tienne in the park when it's still morning? There doesn't seem to be anywhere that is completely secluded, and across the park, she sees two women walking together. Dianne fears she and Tienne will be watched. Dianne fears she and Tienne will *not* be watched. "Over there, that bench behind the two trees. Walk towards that bench. Do you see it?

Nod if you do." Tienne slowly nods her head and feels a rush as the blade scrapes the skin behind her ear.

When they reach the bench, Dianne looks around to see if the other women have noticed them, but they seem oblivious, now walking arm in arm. "I'm going to let go now, don't scream. Just do as I say. Is that clear?" Dianne says. Tienne takes a moment to contemplate the reality of the situation. It has become quite apparent that Dianne intends to fuck her, at knife-point, in a public park in broad daylight. Should she go along with this or should she stop things now while she still can? Sensing her hesitation, Dianne puts the knife to Tienne's throat. "There really is no escape, so either we do this my way, or you get hurt. Do you understand?" As Tienne weakly nods, Dianne pushes her towards the bench and instructs her to kneel down on it, all the while keeping an eye out for the two women.

Tienne does as she is told — waiting, anticipating. She tries hard not to squirm too much as she attempts to position herself so that she isn't too uncomfortable. Of course she realizes that comfort is not the objective here, but concentrating on comfort helps her avoid her instinct to beg Dianne to fuck her. Dianne looks at Tienne in her prone position and her anxiety about being seen passes. She starts to think about the talks she and Tienne have had about knives and the pretext of forced sex. She thinks about their lengthy discussions about marking and about all the ramifications of either of them permanently scarring the other. Dianne stands there looking at Tienne's ass, barely covered by her black cotton skirt with the long slit in the back, and decides she doesn't want to turn back. She wants to fuck Tienne, and if they are being watched, all the better.

Rubbing her ass, Dianne whispers to Tienne, "Tell me, do you like to be fucked in the ass? I know you do." Tienne fights hard not to moan as she listens to Dianne. She tries hard to indulge Dianne in the fantasy even though she is close to cumming with the anticipation of the moment. She really wants Dianne to fuck her and she really needs to submit and obey. "You want me to fuck you?" Dianne continues. "Are you longing to feel my dick in your ass? I know you yearn for me to fuck you until you scream." Tienne is not sure how to respond. If she says yes, she might upset Dianne's role as aggressor. But if she says no, will Dianne think she means it? All Tienne can think to do is not to respond, to feign fear. She jumps and gasps when she feels the slap on her ass. Pulling aside her skirt, Dianne places the cool blade against the flesh of her exposed ass and says, "The next sound you make will cost you." Again, Tienne jumps when she feels the slap, but this time she remembers not to make any noise. "Good girl," Dianne says.

Dianne rubs her ass between each blow and is careful to allow her to feel the edge of the knife. Just as Tienne is getting accustomed to the pain, Dianne stops abruptly and fumbles with the buttons on her jeans. She balances the knife on Tienne's ass and whispers, "Don't move. Don't even breathe until I tell you to. You understand?" Tienne nods and tries hard to obey. Dianne unbuttons the front of her jeans and pulls out her ten-inch, latex cock. She reaches into her pocket, pulls out a small tube of lube, and proceeds to carefully and slowly lubricate her dick while she softly tells Tienne what she is doing.

Once lubricated, Dianne picks up the knife, and lightly scrapes it against Tienne's skin, "Good girl. You know how to follow instructions. You are a good girl. Now I want you to be absolutely still and quiet. I'm going to fuck you in the ass the way you like it. I'm going to slide my dick into your asshole and fuck you deep and hard until you feel like you'll be torn in two. I'll fuck you until you long to scream. But you won't scream, will you?" Tienne shakes her head while trying hard not to plead with her to get on with it and fuck her already. "You remember that you must stay quiet? You remember that any noise on your part will leave me no choice but to cut you, right?" Again she nods her head, only this time she arches her back and offers herself to Dianne.

Tienne almost screams when she feels the force of the slap delivered to her ass. "Listen, bitch, I'm running this show. Don't think you can fool me into being gentle with you just 'cause you try to trick me into thinking you want me. I know your kind. Sluts like you are a dime a dozen. So just be still and silent and I won't be forced to slice your ass." Dianne slaps her once more and traces circles on her ass with the tip of the knife. "You're really close to a nasty scar. Don't make me ruin all this pretty flesh with nasty, painful cuts. Understand?" As Tienne begins to nod she feels a well-lubricated finger in her ass. Dianne probes with one, two, and finally three fingers, watching Tienne's ass for signs of any tensing. As she fucks her with her fingers, she says, "You like this, don't you? You like the feel of my fingers pushing into your tight ass. You need more, don't you? You want me to put my whole hand into your ass. You want me to open you up completely, don't you? Don't you, bitch? Answer me!"

Tienne is about to speak when she remembers that she was told to stay silent. With the knife in hand, Dianne grabs a handful of her hair and continues to fuck her with the other hand. Dianne speaks through clenched teeth, "Make up your mind, bitch. You like it, don't you?" As Tienne nods, Dianne lets go of her hair and runs the edge of the knife down the centre of her back. Her blouse and the skin underneath give way while the blood follows the path of the knife. The pain on her back is quickly replaced by the pleasure in her cunt as Dianne slowly slides her dildo into Tienne's trembling ass. Struggling desperately not to make any noise or move, Tienne swallows the last of her fear and apprehension about being fucked in a public place. She uses all of her willpower to silently enjoy the sensation of Dianne fucking her. Dianne fucks her hard and fast and deep. She pulls at her hair; she makes a number of little cuts on her ass where the knife presses between her hand and Tienne's skin.

The two are so engrossed that neither see the other two women, who are now watching them intently, moving closer for a better look. Dianne and Tienne fail to notice one of the women grab the hair of the other and jam her tongue into her mouth. They don't see the strangers grope each other while they watch the scene.

Tienne grips the edge of the bench and bites hard into her own arm to silence her screams as she explodes into orgasm, sending Dianne into her own intense ejaculation. As Tienne cums, Dianne carves her initial into Tienne's right butt cheek, pulls out her hard dick strapped to her throbbing pussy, and tucks it back into her sweat-soaked jeans. She takes an alcohol-soaked cloth from the plastic bag in her pocket and tenderly wipes the blood from Tienne's wounds. She then straightens Tienne's skirt, helps her to her feet, and steadies her as she stumbles. With a supportive hand on the small of Tienne's back, she whispers in Tienne's ear, "I'm taking you home. Don't look back." Tienne nods and obeys.

'73 NOVA

Diana Cage

Roy is a consummate ass chaser. Pussy, snatch, cunt, call it what you will, she wants to fill it, fuck it, stuff it until it breaks — that's her deal. I like it when she holds me down. She's the first girl I've let fuck me like that. Others have tried, but their hearts weren't in it. What I want in bed is to please my lover. And nothing gives Roy a bigger hard-on than a girl who's all tied up and wriggling and wet.

The other night, she picked me up in her egowagon. The Nova. She bought it in So Cal and had it painted down there at Earl Scheib for $99.95 before driving it home to San Francisco. It's bright orange. She's in love with it. It's a '73, with white racing stripes and an off-white vinyl interior.

Since she bought it, her sexual drives have shifted, perverted.

As if she wanted to prove this, as soon as I said "Hello," she said, "I don't give a shit about girls anymore. Now that I have this, I just want to drive it around and wash it and park in it. I want to live in it. I might sleep in it tonight." She then touched the car's body reverently, smoothing her palm over the fender and following the curve. "It's got a little bit of rust on it," she told me, picking at a tiny spot with her finger. "I'll have to get that taken care of." She opened my door and I got in.

"You look sexy. I like those jeans," she said as she climbed behind the wheel.

I was wearing her favourite outfit: stretch jeans, stilettos, a red silk rose barrette in my shoulder-length brown hair. I looked a lot like Cha-Cha, the slutty Catholic girl from *Grease*, the one that Kenickie takes to the school dance when he and Rizzo break up. I guess I'm the slutty Catholic girl. I should send my mom a card thanking her for my perversions

— sex is bad, sex is bad, sex is bad. I wouldn't enjoy getting spanked half as much if I hadn't gone to parochial school.

The Nova's body has sloping lines, like haunches. The back end has muscular thighs. It has a huge backseat, one you can spread out in — Roy is an ass man. I bought her a pink, Vienna sausage-shaped vibrator that plugs into the cigarette lighter. It's not the butchest thing, but I knew she'd enjoy having her orgasms powered by a V8 engine.

I tried to talk her into buying a practical car. I circled ads in the *Auto Trader* for Honda Civics and left it lying on her bed, but she ignored my hints. She pried my thighs apart with her hands, buried her face in my snatch. "I want something big enough to fuck in," she said while lapping lightly at my hardening clit. I didn't want her to own something like the Nova because I knew it would render me powerless to say no. I'm a girl who likes to do just about anything in cars, including, or maybe especially, fucking and drinking.

My dad had a '69 Camaro Rally Sport. Deep purple, paint code 72. We lived in Hawaii. My mom made him sell it because the Hawaii roads were so undeveloped at that time that he never got that V8 out of second gear.

Roy and I talked Chevys on our first date. She's a big girl, thick around the middle, 200 pounds, five-foot-seven. Strong arms in a T-shirt with a picture of The Donnas on it. Her thick curly dark hair is cut close against the sides of her head and a bit longer on the top. She looks like a cross between a fifties greaser and Orson Welles in *The Lady From Shanghai*. Riding around with her reminds me of all the stoner boys I dated in high school. I was hot for any greasy-haired chainsmoker in a Camaro, although I dated one guy who drove a Mustang. We broke up when I began to feel like I was cheating on Chevrolet. I can't really remember any of them individually now; they've all mushed into one big backseat finger fuck blob.

I asked Roy to help me hang some shelves in my new apartment. She likes to help me out around the house. She likes to help me out in other ways too, but the marathon sex sessions cloud my brain. I lose myself in her fist, in her cock. I can't eat or work.

I craved the type of clarity that I feel when my thighs are shut. And I've been sublimating my sexual tension into home improvement projects. We went to Discount Builders for brackets, but building supply stores always scream sex dungeon to me, so while we were there I bought rope. Roy wanted to tie me up. I wanted her to. My brain said, "You don't need that." But my robot arm lifted and pointed to the huge wheels of soft nylon rope and my evil twin's voice asked for twenty feet. The clerk reeled it off. I felt my cunt drip as I added it to the basket. I also bought a drill and screws. I've always wanted a drill. Every year I asked for one for Christmas, and every year I got a bottle of perfume.

When we got home, Roy threw me down on the bed. I pretended to struggle because I know it gets her hot. There was a hole in my ratty cotton panties and she exploited it with her tongue before ripping the crotch out. She fished a pocketknife from her pants and sliced open the elastic. She held my hands above my head as she slipped her cock into my sopping cunt. "Please let me come, baby. Please," I said, almost too quickly. "Please let me come" actually means "please fuck me hard." Roy figured this out right away.

"Jesus fucking Christ," said Roy.

She fucked me hard, her huge cock sliding in and out of my burning cunt. The pressure was so great, it was almost painful. I tried to slow her down as I got closer and closer because I was afraid. I wanted to come, but I was afraid to end it. I couldn't hold back.

"You're a fucking slut for my cock, aren't you?" she said. She wrapped her fist in my hair and yanked my head back so hard I couldn't answer her. The questions are rhetorical anyway.

My pussy felt like it was on fire — a long, fiery chamber of pressure and friction and heat. Finally, I rolled through a long orgasm, feeling as if I had been turned inside out. Roy slipped her fingers behind the big silicone dick that she covets so much. Her strokes slowed as she flogged her clit with the same urgency she had just had for my cunt. She pushed into me deeper and slower, using my tight muscles as leverage to increase the pressure of her fingers on her clit. I whispered all my secrets to her. I murmured all my loving words.

"God, I love your body," she said. "I love you like this."

Her thrusting ceased and she pushed her cock in all the way, as far as it would go. I could feel her fingers going faster and faster. The thought of her coming was almost too much to bear. I felt like a giant gaping hole, as if I would never be full enough.

After sex, I felt sad. It's not that I don't love her, because I do. And it's not that I need love in order to fuck, because I don't. But I hate losing all control like that. I don't want to need it. I don't want to feel that pleasepleaseplease. My life clouds over, goes soft focus. Everything takes on a gauzy haze, like Farrah Fawcett in *Playboy*. When I came, I felt like the sex negatives in *Café Flesh*, suffering from psychological torment in a post-apocalyptic society of constant sexual desire with no physical outlet. Every time a girl fucks me, I feel like she should have to pay for me and take me home.

As penance, Roy and I went to IKEA to buy another shelf. It was Friday night around seven, and the Bay Bridge was clogged up. We were stopped in traffic listening to Credence Clearwater Revival on her AM radio.

"Hand me that vibrator," Roy said all of a sudden.

I pictured her in the throes of an orgasm, careening blindly into oncoming traffic. Amidst the wreckage, the auto vibe. I'd go down in history.

"We're barely moving," Roy said.

I dug around in the glove compartment until I found the Auto Vibe and unreeled the cord. It thrummed as I plugged it in.

The people in the cars next to us looked bored. They had work clothes on, suits and ties. "Cars should come standard with these, for relaxed commuting," Roy said as she unbuckled her belt.

The vibrator buzzed for a few moments and we said nothing to each other. Finally, Roy broke in with, "Tell me a dirty story,"

"I can't think of anything right now."

"Come on," she said. "Just make up something."

"OK, OK," I said. I did really want to help out. "I'll try. Let's see."

I mentally thumbed through the cache of smutty fantasies I routinely tell Roy to get her hot until I found something suitable. "So you're driving down 5 on the way to Los Angeles. You've got a car boner. It's straining against your 501s. Eighties hair-rock queen Lita Ford drives up beside you. She's wearing a tight, hot pink leather miniskirt and pumps. She spots you too. She knows you've got a monster in your pants and she wants it. So she signals for you to pull over at the next rest stop."

"Uh-huh. Yeah," said Roy.

"She wants to suck that big cock of yours."

"Yeah, she does," said Roy.

My heart was not in the story, so my timing was off. I started rushing the events. I kept getting to the end of the fantasy before Roy got off and then I'd have to start over with a new version. After Roy fucked Lita Ford over the sink in the rest stop bathroom a few times, I started putting myself into the story. It got confusing, because part of the time I was Lita Ford, and part of the time I was screwing Lita Ford.

Just when I was propping Lita up on the imaginary rest stop bathroom to eat her out, Roy pulled off the freeway and screeched into the IKEA parking lot. She sped towards the back, one hand on the steering wheel and one in her pants, parking spastically across several spaces. Then she cut the engine and concentrated on coming. I whispered the rest of the story into her ear, in breathy little chunks punctuated by the words cock and cunt, repeated over and over. The story was ridiculous by then, involving several highway patrol officers and a gang of truckers, like a scene from *Smokey and the Bandit*. My sexual fantasies are always extravagant. When I was a kid, my Barbie was either getting gang-banged by pirates, or having her penthouse taken over by Confederate soldiers, who would force her to cook and clean and service them sexually, which she'd do for the love of her country.

Roy finally came, and immediately discarded the Auto Vibe like it was the wrapper on a Whopper Junior. She buckled her belt and said, "Let's go."

I got out of the car, feeling overheated and sticky. I felt distant from her. The store was full of lesbians, but they all looked married and suburban, and not in a dirty, wife-swapping party way.

Roy gestured toward a nearly naked young woman in the bathroom linen section. "How old do you think she is?" Roy asked. "Twenty?" The girl was straight out of a Britney Spears video — scantily clad and gazing absently at the bathroom mats. Roy and I pretended to be interested in a shower curtain with little bubbles all over it while we surreptitiously checked out her ass. I felt predatory and creepy, like Mercedes McCambridge in *Touch of Evil*, in the scene where she rapes Janet Leigh. When her mom spotted us, I said, "This is too weird." Roy agreed. We paid for the shelf and lumbered back out to the parking lot like the zombies in *Dawn of the Dead*.

The totally empty lot was so expansive and dark, and Roy was so torqued up from our stalking adventure, that she couldn't resist pulling a few donuts with the Nova. I was totally unprepared for doing donuts in the IKEA parking lot. How do you prepare for that exactly? So I screamed at the top of my lungs like I was on an amusement park ride. She screeched around as fast as she could, leaving a long black rubber streak on the asphalt. The flashing red light behind us told me we were in trouble. "Uh-oh," I said.

Two cops got out of their car and yelled at us the top of their lungs, just like TV cops. It was exciting at first because it felt like we actually were on TV. But when they continued to scream at us without really taking a breath, I got worried for them. One of the cops was purple and had a bulging vein in his forehead.

"What is your problem, buddy?" asked cop number one. "What the fuck do you think you're doing?"

"I'm gonna take you in and impound your car, asshole," said cop number two. He was tapping on the car door with his nightstick which, to be honest, was kind of hot. But also terrifying. He thought Roy was a guy.

Roy was handling the situation well, being polite, and handing the cop her licence, remaining calm. But everything was moving slowly and I suddenly felt like I had to step in and clear up his incorrect pronoun usage. I really don't like to be mistaken for straight.

"She was just trying to scare me, officer," I said in my sweetest voice; being sweet and helpless to cops used to work well for me in South Carolina where I grew up. Sadly, the few times I've tried in San Francisco, it's backfired and gotten me tickets.

The cop butched up. "Lady, he needs to realize that what he did is a felony, not just a traffic ticket. He could have smeared some poor little kid all over the road."

"I said *she*," I said, correcting his pronoun.

"Does he realize he could go to jail?" the cop continued.

"*She*," I repeated. Then there was a pregnant pause in the conversation, during which the officer shone his Maglight onto Roy's cute boy face for a long time. Finally, he said, "Excuse me," sounding very confused. I don't know what switched on in his brain once he realized we were two women. It seemed that he suddenly felt like he was involved in something they hadn't covered in cop school. His entire demeanor changed. He actually became polite, almost calm. "OK," he said. "I'm not going to give you a ticket. But I want you to drive out of this parking lot like a little old lady."

"Thank you, officer," said Roy in her best little-old-lady voice. And then we drove off, like little old ladies.

The Nova's enormous size was impressive. You could easily sit three in the front. I leaned against the passenger door, heart still palpitating from getting yelled at by the police. I was also so turned on. My panties were soaked. I squeezed my thighs together and concentrated on the throb in my clit. It felt like a marble. It ached. Roy and I were very far away from each other. I was conscious of the empty space between us. I felt like we had to yell to hear each other.

"I'm going to stop and get gas," Roy yelled.

"OK," I yelled back.

While she gassed up the car, I watched the gallons click off on the gas pump. Twelve, thirteen, fourteen, fifteen. The thing must have a twenty-gallon tank. The capacity impressed me; I think of her gas tank as a cavernous cunt. I wanted to put my fist in it.

When she squealed out of the gas station, anger rose up the back of my neck with prickly redness. Sometimes Roy's insistence on having this thing that I don't have: a big engine, speed, power, a cock, makes me angry. When we take off our clothes, we both have the same fucking hole, though you wouldn't know it if you heard us talking about sex. We talk about her cock and my cunt so often, that when we're naked and there are two cunts, I get cognitive disonance.

As though responding to me, Roy said, "Do you hate my driving?"

"Yeah, you drive like a dick," I said.

Contributor Biographies

Diana Cage is the editor of *On Our Backs* magazine, and the author of *Box Lunch: The Layperson's Guide to Cunnilingus* (Alyson Books). Her most recent book is the collection *Bottoms Up: Writing About Sex* (Soft Skull Press). You can read more about her work at *www.dianacage.com*.

Anna Camilleri is a writer and spoken word artist who lives in Toronto. She authored *I Am a Red Dress* (Arsenal Pulp Press). Her next book, *Red Light: Superheroes, Saints, and Sluts* is an anthology that explores new interpretations of female icons. Anna co-edited *Brazen Femme* (Arsenal Pulp Press), which was shortlisted for a Lambda Literary Award, and co-founded Taste This, a spoken word performance troupe that collaborated to publish the critically acclaimed *Boys Like Her* (Press Gang). Anna can be contacted at *www.annacamilleri.com*. Note: An earlier version of "Prism" appeared in *I Am a Red Dress*, as "Topsoil, Aftershave, and Charm."

rp chow used to be androgynous in the late 1980s and butchy-femme in the 1990s, but now resides in an uncertain, XX gender frame from which she writes and lives in Vancouver.

Ducky DooLittle's story is one of a woman who emerged from behind the peepshow glass to the head of the class — as one of America's most celebrated sex educators. She spent her teenage years in New York City working as a 42nd Street peepshow girl. She would use her daily grind as grist for her tantalizing tales which would in time be published in erotic literary journals, fashion magazines, and cut-rate, glossy porno mags. Her written work later jumped from the page to the stage. Today she is a sex educator, writer, and comedian. Her website is www.duckydoolittle. com.

Miss Kitty Galore is a saucy, bossy, Macho Femme, a.k.a. Kristyn Dunnion, author of children's novel *Missing Matthew* (Red Deer Press); *Mosh Pit*, her second book, is queer, punkrawk teen fiction (Red Deer Press).

She has stories in *Geeks, Misfits and Outlaws* (McGilligan Press), *Ana-coenesis I & II* (Trade Queer Things), and the young adult anthology, *The Horrors I* (Red Deer Press). She likes big boots, shaved heads, loud music, and lipstick.

San Francisco-based poet **Daphne Gottlieb** stitches together the ivory tower and the gutter using just her tongue. She is the author of three books of poetry: *Final Girl* (Soft Skull Press), *Why Things Burn* (Soft Skull Press), and *Pelt* (Odd Girls Press), with a fourth, *Kissing Dead Girls*, in progress. She was the winner of the 2003 Audre Lorde Award for Poetry and a 2001 Firecracker Alternative Book Award. She is also the editor of the forthcoming *Homewrecker: An Adultery Reader* (Soft Skull Press) and is currently at work on a graphic novel with illustrator Diane DiMassa. You can find her online at *www.daphnegottlieb.com*.

Sara Graefe is a Vancouver-based femme-scribe. An award-winning playwright and screenwriter, she also writes hot little stories to make her girlfriend wet. Her short fiction has appeared in feminist and lesbian anthologies such as *Seven Sisters* (Seven Sisters Writing Group), *Lady Driven* (Permanent Press), and *Hot & Bothered 4* (Arsenal Pulp Press).

Nalo Hopkinson's mother is increasingly alarmed by the sexual content of her writing, so that's probably all to the good. Nalo is the author of *Brown Girl in the Ring*, *Midnight Robber*, and *Skin Folk*, all published by Warner Aspect Books, and *Salt Roads* (Warner Books), and co-editor of *So Long Been Dreaming: Postcolonial Science Fiction and Fantasy* (Arsenal Pulp Press). Born in Jamaica, Nalo moved to Canada when she was sixteen. She lives in Toronto. An extended version of this story was originally published in her short story collection, *Skin Folk*.

Rachel Kramer Bussel edited *Naughty Spanking Stories from A to Z* 1 and 2 (Pretty Things Press), among others. She is Senior Editor at *Penthouse Variations* and writes the "Lusty Lady" column in *The Village Voice*. Her writing has been published in *Bust, Curve, Diva, On Our Backs, Penthouse, Punk Planet, Rockrgrl*, and many erotic anthologies. Her website is *www.rachelkramerbussel.com*.

Leah Lakshmi Piepzna-Samarasinha is a U.S.-raised, Toronto-based, queer Sri Lankan writer and spoken word artist. The author of *Consensual Genocide* (TSAR), her writing has been published in *Colonize This!* (Seal Press), *Dangerous Families* (Harrington Park Press), *Brazen Femme* (Arsenal Pulp Press), *Without a Net*, and *Geeks, Misfits and Outlaws* (McGilligan Books), *Lodestar Quarterly, Mizna, SAMAR, Bamboo Girl, Bitch,* and *Colorlines.* She likes riding her adult trike in short skirts with the CRANKY BROWN QUEER GIRL AGAINST WAR sign.

Miss Cookie LaWhore is Michael V. Smith. A poet, zinester, comedian, filmmaker, sex artist, and occasional clown, Smith is an MFA grad from the University of British Columbia's Creative Writing program. Smith's novel, *Cumberland* (Cormorant Books), was nominated for the *Amazon.ca* Books in Canada First Novel Award. In 2004, Smith won the Western Magazine Award for Fiction, the Audience Choice Award for Best Short Film at Vancouver's Out On Screen, and was nominated for the Journey Prize. Find out more at *www.michaelvsmith.com.*

Suki Lee is the author of *Sapphic Traffic* (Conundrum Press), a collection of cross-continental, pulp-inspired short stories. Her fiction appeared previously in the Arsenal Pulp Press anthologies, *Hot & Bothered 3* and *4.* Originally from Montréal, Suki now lives in Ottawa where she is working on a novel. Her website is *www.sukilee.com.*

May Lui is a mixed-race writer and activist living in Toronto. This is her first time having erotica/porn published and she's very excited! In addition to writing, she loves cats, chocolate, anti-racist theory, and deep, intense, passionate connections.

Elaine Miller is a Vancouver leatherdyke who spends her time playing, learning, educating, performing, and writing. Since 1994, her work has appeared in numerous magazines, anthologies, and quite a few tawdry porn sites. Also, she is the bdsm/kink columnist for *Xtra! West* newspaper. She's also a bit of a geek: *www.elainemiller.com.*

Sherece Taffe is a writer and book artist currently working and living in

Toronto. She creates bookworks by hand. Designing, writing, printing, and binding allows her to play with a medium that reveals a message as well as being the message. "Knifed" appeared in the 1996 summer/fall issue of *DaJuice!: A Black Lesbian Thang*.

Zoe Whittall is the author of *The Best Ten Minutes of Your Life* and the editor of *Geeks, Misfits and Outlaws* (McGilligan Books). Her creative work has been anthologized widely in books like *Breathing Fire 2: Canada's New Poets* (Nightwood Editions), *Girls Who Bite Back* (Sumach Press), *Brazen Femme: Queering Femininity* (Arsenal Pulp Press), and more. She is also one-third of the high femme performance art troupe, Trash and Ready. She lives in Toronto.

Amber Dawn is a Vancouver-based writer, performance artist, and radical sex/gender activist. In 2004, she performed in the Sex Workers' Art Show, which toured twenty-three American cities. She is co-editor, creator, and actor in *Girl on Girl*, an award-winning sex documentary which has screened at international film festivals. Her poems have been published in both Canadian and U.S. literary magazines.

Trish Kelly is the author of more than twenty chapbooks and zines, including the well-known series, *The Make Out Club*. She is a contributor to CBC Radio and has had her work anthologized in *Hot & Bothered 4* (Arsenal Pulp Press), *Quickies 3* (Arsenal Pulp Press), *Glamour Girls: Femme/Femme Erotica* (Haworth Press), and *How To Fuck a Tranny*.